'Who were we?' is book 3 i

Book 1) Abduction Inspired UFO Disclosure is only the Start

Book 2) The Void

Book 3) Who were we?

Main Characters

Jenny Quinn (Sarah Aston)

Natalie James (Lara Hine)

Synopsis

Who were we starts from where The Void left off. Jenny Quinn and Natalie James have only just laid eyes on one another and yet they are already in-love and are profoundly aware of a cosmic connection they have crossing time and space. But how much of this can they remember? And to what lengths would they go to discover a fix if something were to harm their connection to one another in this life?

1. Looking in the eyes of love

The year is 2056. Jenny Quinn and Natalie James exit Grand Central train station but they do not go their separate ways. They go to Jenny's Brooklyn apartment. They have a romantic candle-lit dinner with the late 20th century/early 21st century Irish band, the Corrs playing in the background. Both Jenny and Natalie are experiencing mixed feelings on the issue of whether or not this is love at first sight. Because they have only just met but they feel as if they have known each other intimately for centuries.

Jenny has prepared Spaghetti carbonara. The drink is Chardonnay wine.

"What is the music in the background?" asks Natalie.

"They are an old Irish band. The Corrs."

"Not heard of them. Beautiful song choice though. The lyrics are perfect for this moment."

https://www.youtube.com/watch?v=-2_lNxjxLmQ

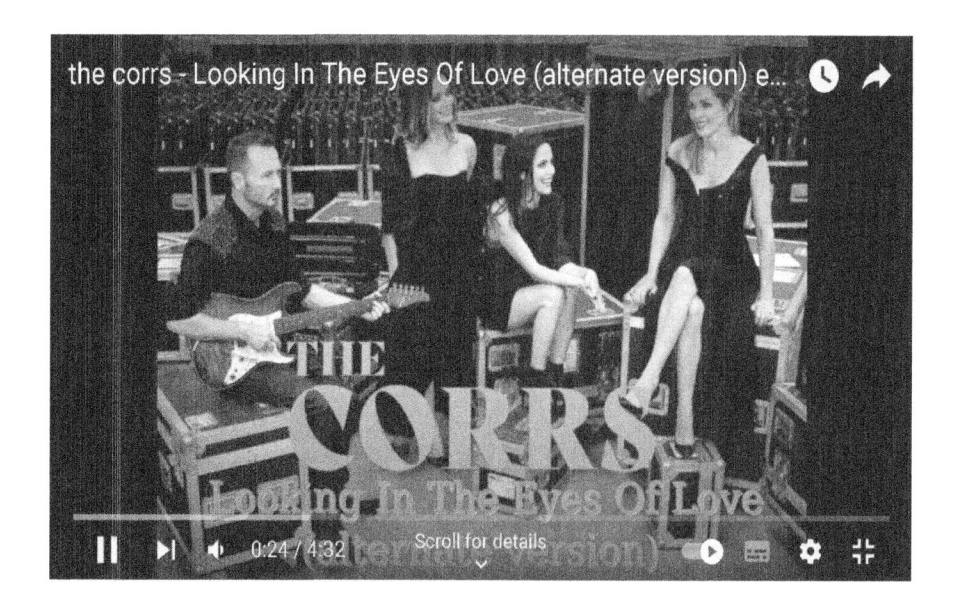

"I'm an Irish New Yorker on my mother's side and she was more Irish than American in my view."

Both Jenny and Natalie are experiencing a profoundly strong connection and find it hard to know what else to say other than making that point. On the one hand it is the greatest feeling each woman has ever experienced. On the other hand it is frustrating and uncomfortable as they are lost for words.

"We are deflecting from what we really want to talk about."

"Yeah, I know."

"I mean, I know you."

"I know you too."

"But who are you?… I mean… oh I can't say the words."

"I am Jenny." Jenny pauses trying to think of what Natalie means by her question. But its unanswerable because Natalie isn't referring to this life. Jenny goes to speak but stops, feeling a complete mental block."

"I…"

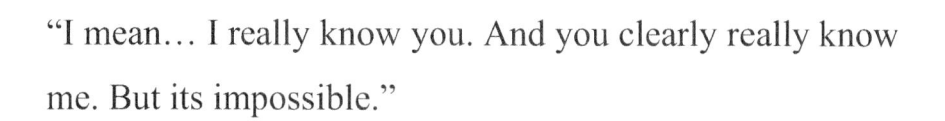

"I mean… I really know you. And you clearly really know me. But its impossible."

"Not in this life. But I feel all of it too. Believe me Natalie. There's empathy on steroids here." replies Jenny.

Natalie stares into Jenny's eyes and says "I can feel things that were once felt concerning us but I cannot put any other type of memory to it, of place or an event. But being in love with you is always there… or at least wanting you."

"Again, I sense and feel all of that too."

"Does your work on Simulation tell you anything?"

"No it doesn't unfortunately. This, meaning you Natalie, feels so personal. My work on the other hand doesn't feel personal... Not to this degree anyway. This is profoundly personal."

"But if we remember how we felt and understand that we are connected, then this provides us with hope that memories will surface into consciousness."

Jenny smiles… and says "Exactly, that is what I am passionately hoping will happen."

Jenny and Natalie finish their meal and are now enjoying the Chardonnay wine. Jenny asks to see an example of one of Natalie's short stories. Using augmented reality. Natalie makes her short story appear right before their eyes in mid air. She says

"Augmented. Show me the book called Stalker by Natalie James."

"There you go Jenny."

"Give me an overview of the story arc."

"It is about a man called Mike who stalks a woman called Lara after Lara steals his wife off him. He cannot handle the injustice of it all and he goes insane. He started off rather boring but ended up with an all consuming blood boiling hatred that destroyed himself. He follows Lara and his ex wife to a lakeside cottage. He manages to tie his ex up and set the Lakeside cottage on fire. The ex dies in the fire. And he comes extremely close to murdering Lara. He very nearly started to throw punches at her. But despite the isolated location of the cottage there was a couple, who are in love, who like to come here to walk the dog and in this case for not only walking their dog, but also romantically resting afterwards and drinking summer wine on the grass.

But while walking their dog they observe that something is kicking off in the distance… luckily for Lara, the woman, Sarah, is brave enough to intervene when she realizes that Lara is in danger. She saves Lara's life by smashing Mike over the head with a wine bottle that Sarah had with her. Her boyfriend had tried to persuade her not to intervene but she did anyway. In the short story Lara and Sarah end up together after the boyfriend ditches his girlfriend as he doesn't want the grief of being with someone who will be accused by some people of murder."

Natalie hasn't quite finished her story overview but she stops as she notices tears in Jenny's eyes.

"What's the matter?"

"The name Lara. You are Lara. You have done some crazy things" says Jenny while tears of love fall from her eyes.

2. Dreams and DMT

Darkness surrounds Lara. She cannot see anything. All is blackness. Where am I? Is anyone else here? Is anything else here? Am I completely alone? Then she hears a female voice saying "I will never leave you Lara." Lara looks around but see's no-one. She calls out "WHERE ARE YOU SARAH?" Her eyes suddenly open. She had been dreaming but in the dream she was Lara and she called out to Jenny... except she called her Sarah.

"Sarah, wake up." Natalie (or Lara) nudges the woman she already regards as her lover.

Jenny wakes up and instantly says "Sarah?"

Lara strokes her lovers hair. There are tears in her eyes. She whispers "I had a dream. I remembered you. You are Sarah."

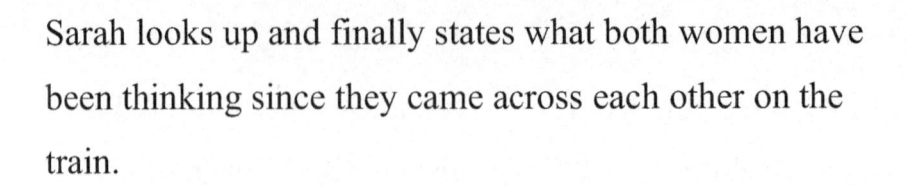

Sarah looks up and finally states what both women have been thinking since they came across each other on the train.

"We are reincarnated."

Again they are wiping the tears from their eyes.

"We need to stop crying Sarah."

"How can we with this realization. Its miraculous and its beautiful."

Lara does what Lara does in emotional situations. She goes to fetch a wine. She comes back pouring two glasses. Through tears she says

"You have been swimming in my head all of my life. I wrote stories about us. You write academic papers about the Simulated Universe. I write about us in short stories in all kinds of simulated environments. I used the name Lara as my central character more than any other name."

"Well, Lara. Who were we? I mean we know our first names. But not our second names. We know very little. Clearly we were in love. But what were our jobs or careers?"

"Do you have any hunches?"

"Yes. You got up to some crazy things. Maybe I did too given that we were clearly in-love."

"Lara is a schemer" replies Natalie referring to how she often writes about her in fiction.

"I want to lend all of your fictional books. Or at least all of those that you think refer to us."

Lara nods and then asks "So am I Natalie or Lara? Am I Lara with you and Natalie with everyone else. And are you Jenny or Sarah?"

"What is your answer to that Lara?"

"Nice way to answer a question with a question. I don't know Sarah. But seriously, you are Sarah to me but obviously you are Jenny to everyone else."

"Well, I hope to one day come out as Sarah. But I want to remember my second name first."

"Any ideas for how we find answers?"

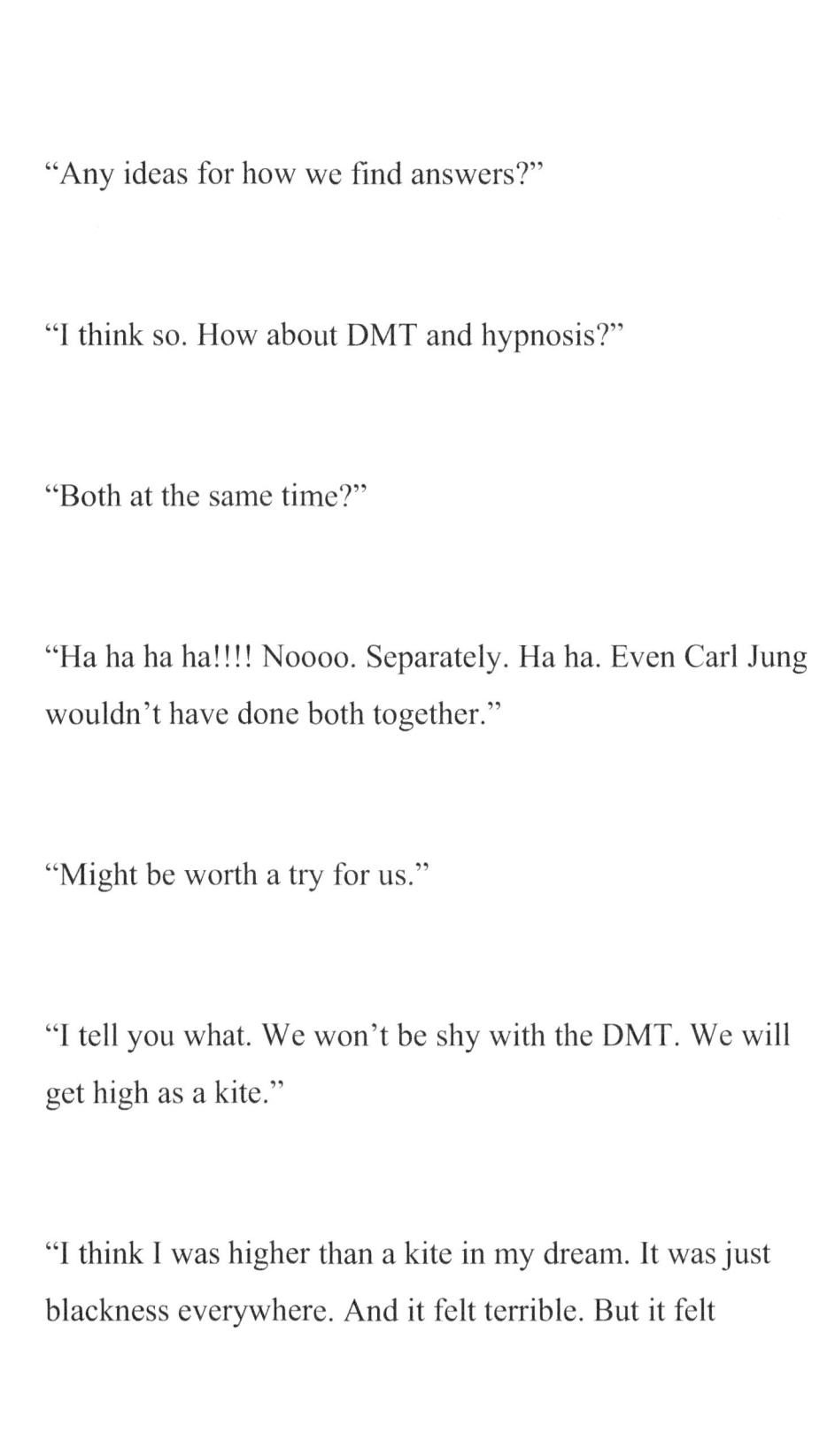

"I think so. How about DMT and hypnosis?"

"Both at the same time?"

"Ha ha ha ha!!!! Noooo. Separately. Ha ha. Even Carl Jung wouldn't have done both together."

"Might be worth a try for us."

"I tell you what. We won't be shy with the DMT. We will get high as a kite."

"I think I was higher than a kite in my dream. It was just blackness everywhere. And it felt terrible. But it felt somehow familiar as well. It felt like a real place. Does absolute blackness mean anything to you Sarah?"

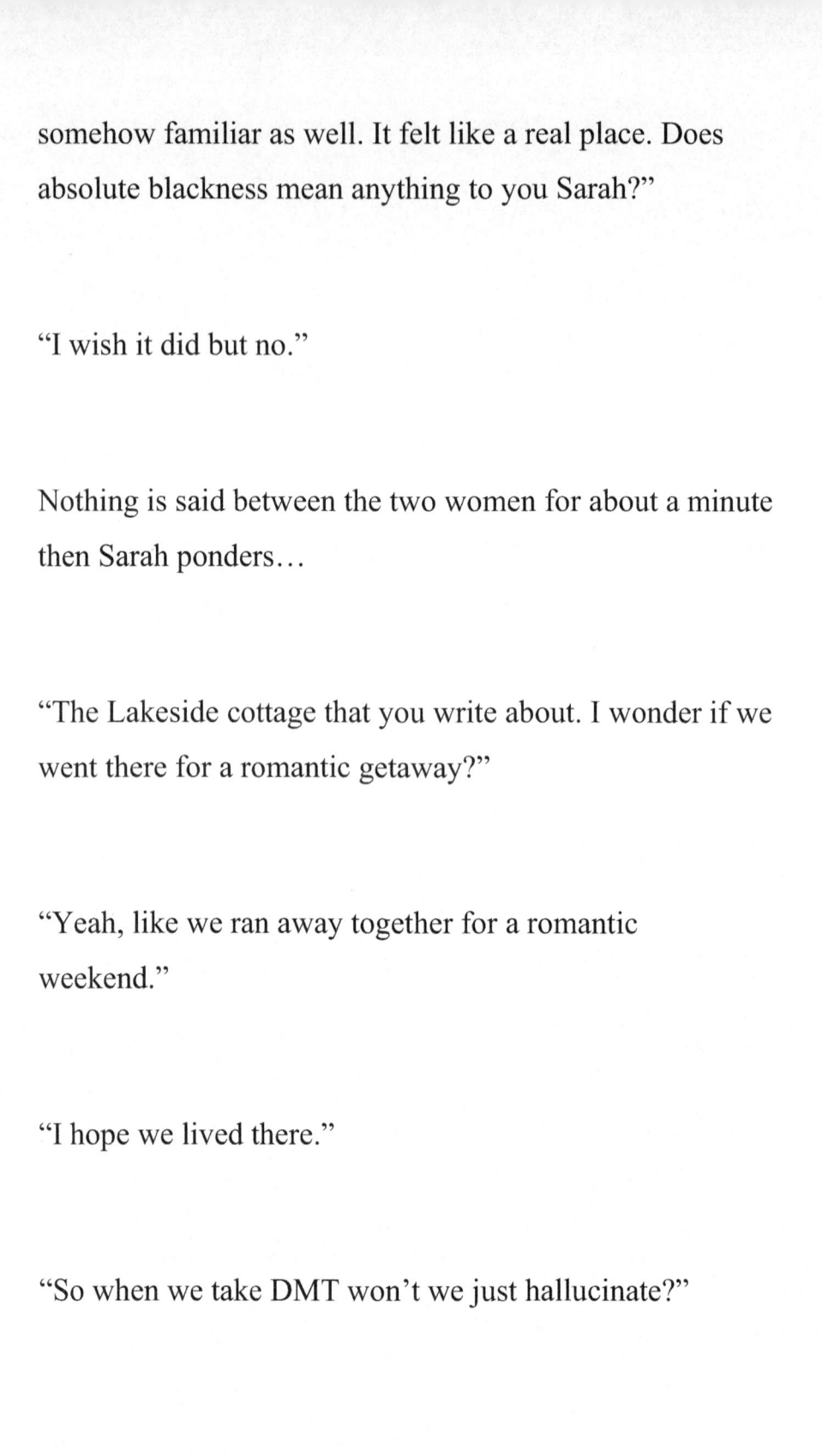

"I wish it did but no."

Nothing is said between the two women for about a minute then Sarah ponders…

"The Lakeside cottage that you write about. I wonder if we went there for a romantic getaway?"

"Yeah, like we ran away together for a romantic weekend."

"I hope we lived there."

"So when we take DMT won't we just hallucinate?"

"Yes. But its about opening up our minds. It might help. It might have a psychological impact breaking through layers of amnesia."

"I am so happy."

"Good. Tomorrow night you shall be saying… I am so high."

The next morning Lara stayed at Sarah's home while Sarah went out and booked a private hypnosis session for her and Lara later for later in the week. Lara re-read some of her own work but nothing from previous lives surfaced to consciousness. But when she looked through the music collection of Sarah's a near century old song caught her attention. She played it.

https://www.youtube.com/watch?v=8LhkyyCvUHk

But Lara wondered if she was clutching at straws and trying to convince herself of almost anything. She thought that the song would have been before her and Sarah's time even in a previous life… as Lara was thinking linearly.

DMT Time! Sarah and Lara are smoking from a pipe. Both women see the world around them seemingly melt. Then meticulously brilliant archetypal patterns appear before their very eyes. Moments later and Lara is seeing gnomes. And she meets a princess.

"Am I reincarnated?" asks Lara.

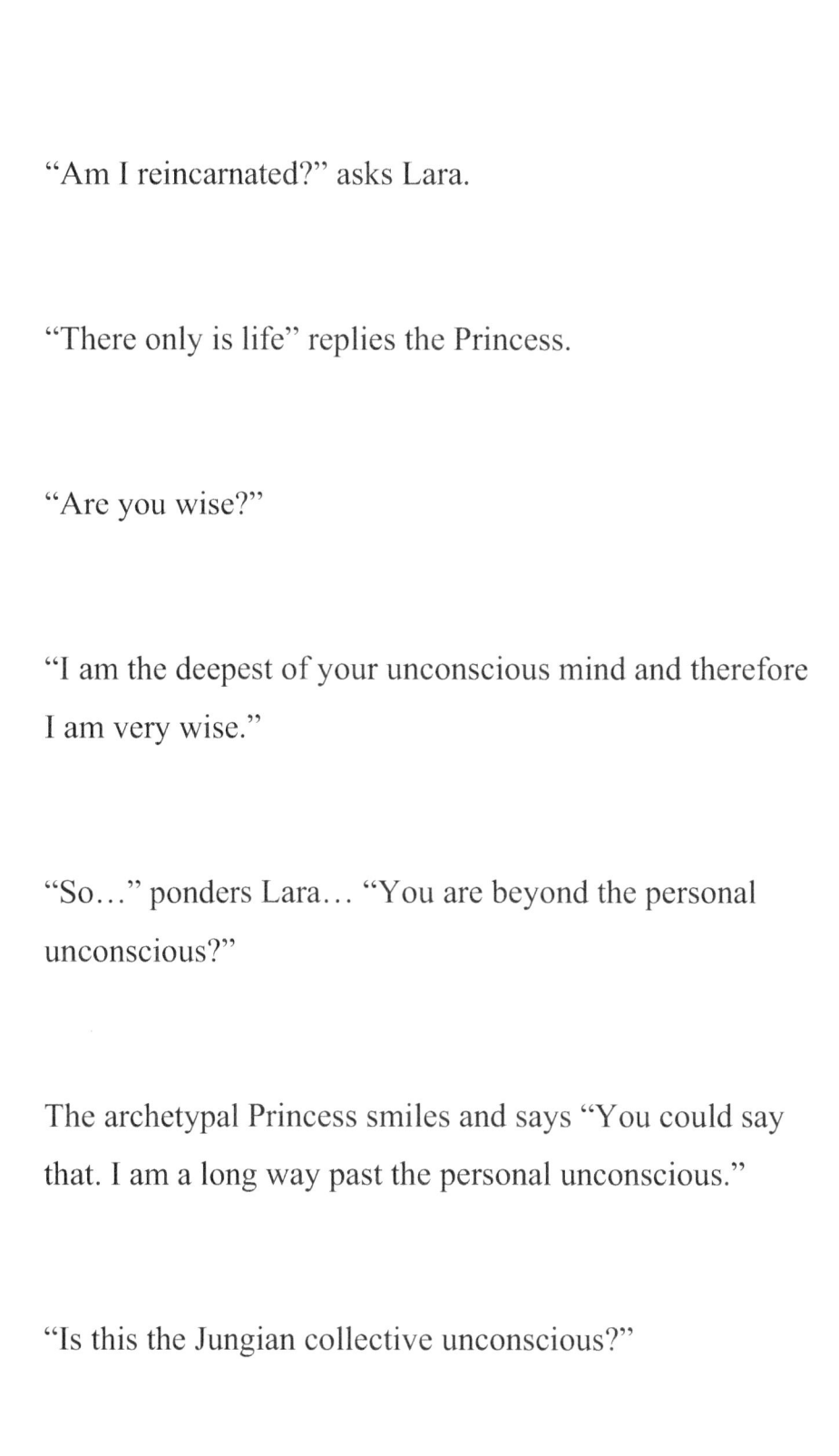

"There only is life" replies the Princess.

"Are you wise?"

"I am the deepest of your unconscious mind and therefore I am very wise."

"So…" ponders Lara… "You are beyond the personal unconscious?"

The archetypal Princess smiles and says "You could say that. I am a long way past the personal unconscious."

"Is this the Jungian collective unconscious?"

"Yes. But it goes deeper than Jung ever dared to go."

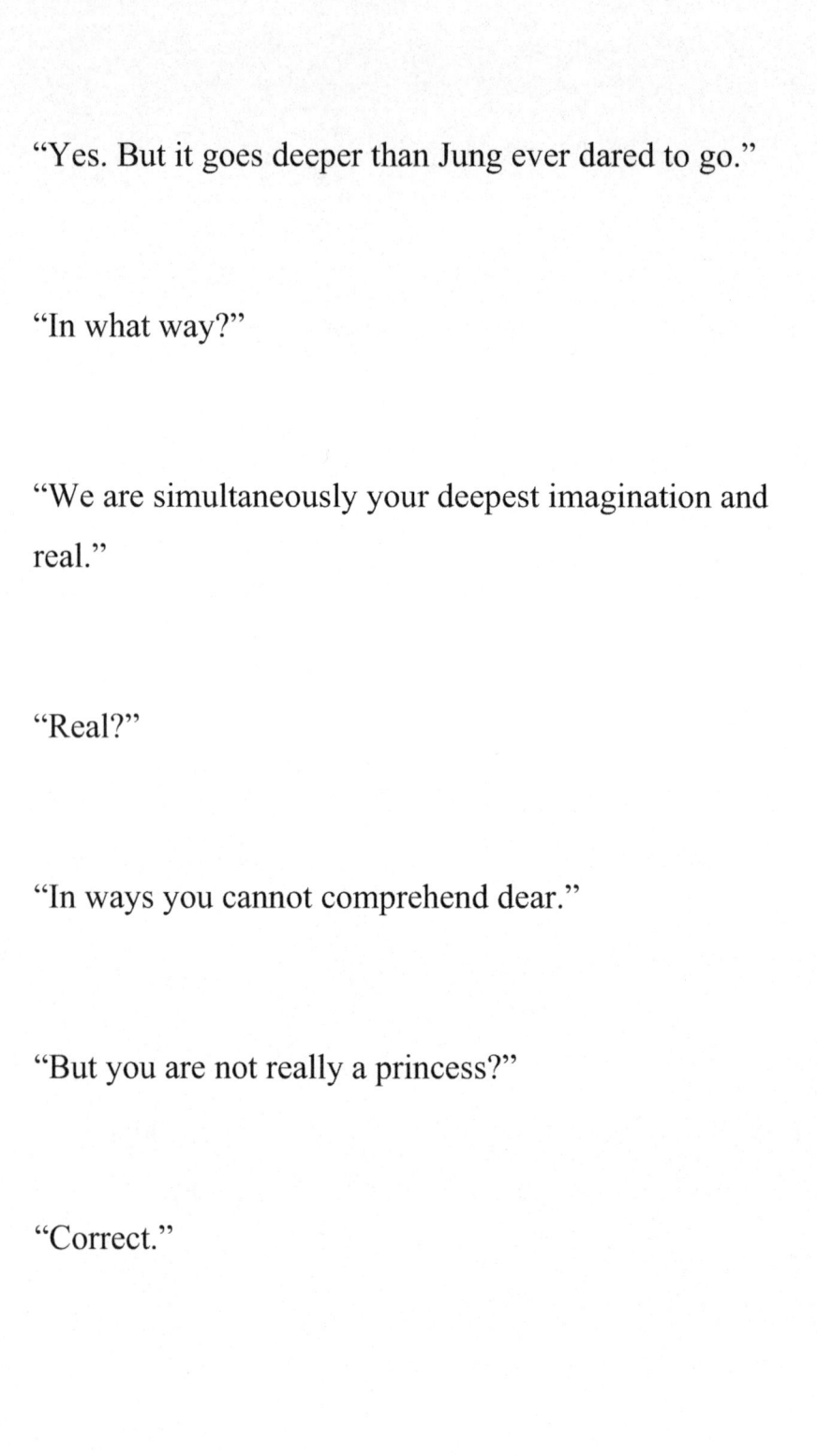

"In what way?"

"We are simultaneously your deepest imagination and real."

"Real?"

"In ways you cannot comprehend dear."

"But you are not really a princess?"

"Correct."

"So what are you?"

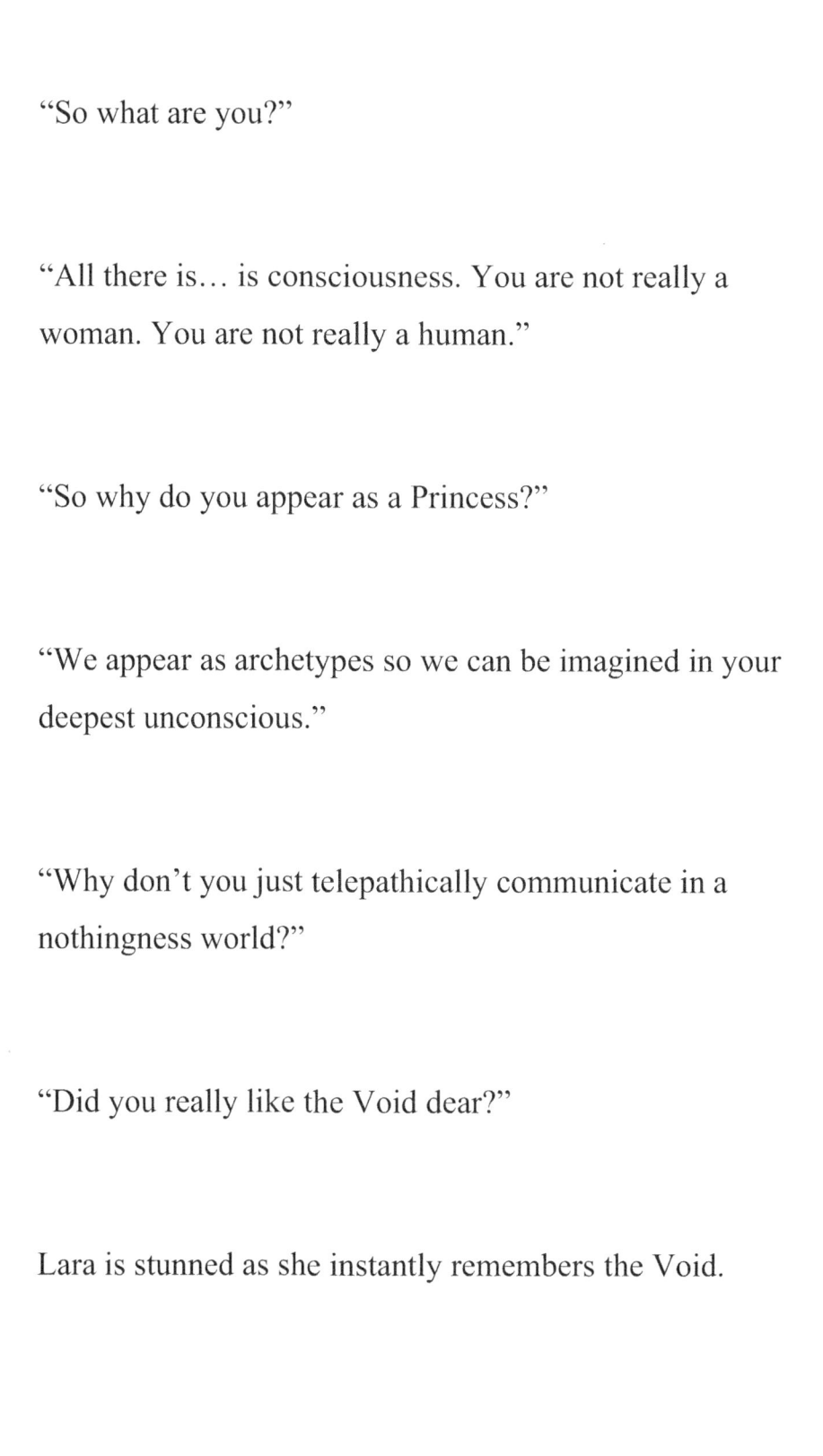

"All there is… is consciousness. You are not really a woman. You are not really a human."

"So why do you appear as a Princess?"

"We appear as archetypes so we can be imagined in your deepest unconscious."

"Why don't you just telepathically communicate in a nothingness world?"

"Did you really like the Void dear?"

Lara is stunned as she instantly remembers the Void.

Meanwhile Sarah's experience is dominated by UFO's and extraterrestrials. One of the things they communicate to her matches what the Princess told Lara… that all there is… is consciousness.

When the two women come back to everyday reality Lara excitedly informs Sarah that she has remembered the Void. Sarah cannot remember the Void herself but she was told something. Sarah tells Lara that she remembered that their past life involved UFO's.

"UFO's!!!" responds Lara. Because on this timeline they are a myth, so much so that there is no Disclosure movement. UFO belief is no further ahead than fairies on this timeline. Lara continues "Well I did meet gnomes I suppose so I can't talk."

"And we are reincarnated so surely we can be open to UFO's."

"Well did you remember something about UFO's?"

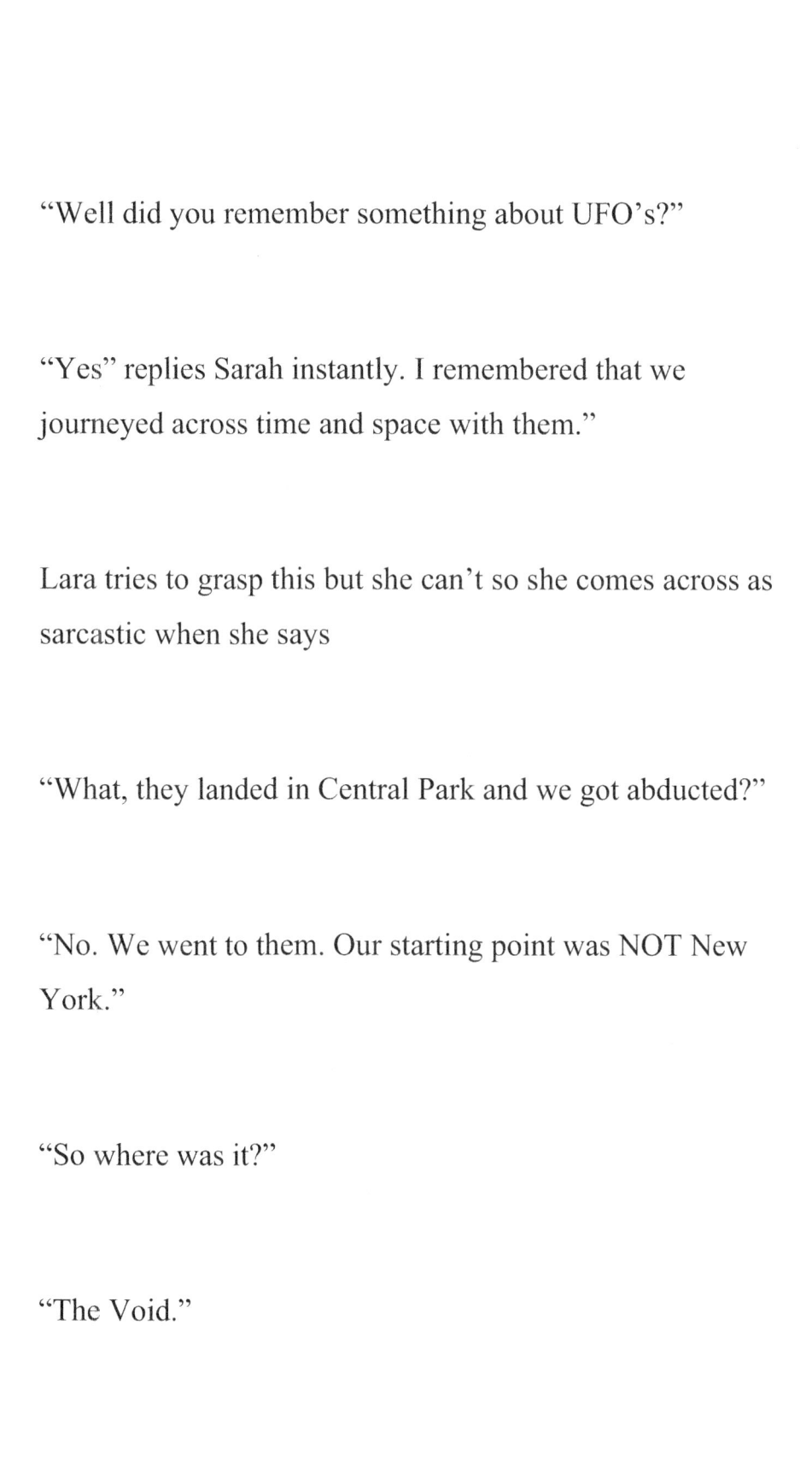

"Yes" replies Sarah instantly. I remembered that we journeyed across time and space with them."

Lara tries to grasp this but she can't so she comes across as sarcastic when she says

"What, they landed in Central Park and we got abducted?"

"No. We went to them. Our starting point was NOT New York."

"So where was it?"

"The Void."

3. False Paths, Huge Progress and being in Love

The following day Sarah went to see a friend whom she had collaborated with on their theories concerning the nature of reality. She parked right outside his house. She got out the car, shut the door but then paused. A negative thought monopolized her mind. It was telling her that their academic theories are nothing compared to the reality of this. This was negative for Sarah because she was feeling like her work was close to worthless. Without value. Without substance. So she got back in the car and went for a coffee instead. Alone with her own thoughts she felt a buzz of anticipation for the hypnosis session coming up tomorrow. Well that's tomorrow sorted out for Sarah. But on the career front she has a problem. That being said, Lara would later remind her that simulation was part of the answer to the puzzle.

The next day Sarah and Lara see the hypnotist called Simon Airey. They introduce themselves as Jenny and Natalie but they openly tell Airey that they consider themselves to be Sarah and Lara.

"What we are trying to do is like the opposite of precognition!" states Sarah.

"We think all is consciousness and that there is just one huge brick wall of repression in the way… resulting in memory loss."

"Well hypnosis can unblock memories. Lets regress you two to previous lives."

"Lives?" responds Lara.

"Well if there can be one previous life, I suppose there can be many more."

"We just want to find out about our connection across time and space, our past life together" says Sarah.

"Ok lets see what we can do."

The hypnosis is a disaster. Nothing is uncovered. Indeed that is the best news about it. The worst news is that Lara felt like she used to really like Michael Jackson's music. Nothing wrong with that except that she didn't. So it led her down a false path. The hypnosis had given her that information because she had heard bits and pieces about his life recently in the media. It was personal unconscious level stuff. The hypnosis was therefore a big disappointment. And on the car journey home things didn't get any better as Sarah argued that if they could discover their second names they could visit their own graves. This is wrong. Sarah and Lara were still alive in 2056. So there is no grave. Moreover they couldn't visit their alive selves in 2056 because they were on a different timeline. So while they were getting things right such as first names, their love for one another, reincarnation, the Void, UFO's journeying across time and space… they were also getting things wrong: Two wrongs were Michael Jackson and thinking they could visit their graves. Other things were vague such as scheming Lara. There is so much they don't know there in terms of her involvement in the Psy-Op that played a huge part in convincing the world of UFO's as our simulators who can also time travel. The irony being that UFO's do time travel but the timeline that Sarah and Lara were interested in did not know that UFOs possessed those abilities but made it up as a Psy-Op. The two women were thinking that simulation is part of the answer and so is consciousness. They already had much of the cosmic reality answer but lacked personal knowledge about their previous life. They were aware of the main personal point that they were lovers but unaware of their life narrative. They were clueless on past family life, clueless that they used to live in Boston and vague on the Lakeside House. Lara had vague feelings of a man who in some way she and Sarah had a love/hate relationship with… but she couldn't really remember Mike Aston... although deep down in her unconscious there must be some type of memory of a Mike as he is right there in her book … 'Stalker'. Lara and Sarah thought that the song Venus had some involvement with their past life and while that is true they were also wondering if Michael Jackson did too? As said, that one is a false path.

"Its so frustrating Lara. We connected instantly and it felt like everything would just flow into our consciousness at once. But now I am worried that we are stuck. We know some things but so much else is missing. Most of our previous life is missing from our consciousness. And there's the risk that one of us may remember more than the other. For instance I don't feel anything about Michael Jackson."

"Isn't this good for your career Sarah? You can now add the Void to the Simulation theory… as part of the

Simulated Universe. You can start to talk about tracking consciousness into the Void and into the next life."

"Maybe. One thing I am thinking about is recording our dreams. The technology now exists. I think I will make a purchase. But I am worried about recalling a past life. I don't see why it comes so strong with the love and connectedness to you but then so much else is an amnesia or is vague."

"I only half agree. We are privileged to have learned so much and to have connected with one another. I think the UFO breakthrough maybe tells us all the key info concerning the nature of reality. UFO's journey across time and space. That means they time travel to wherever and whenever they want. And in the Void you can somehow journey with them. Meaning you go to them. They do not abduct you. I mean that is frigging well profound cosmic knowledge with cherries on top! But I also get what you mean, as a short story writer I want the whole narrative and that includes knowledge about my past personal life."

"Its like those fictional stories about blacked out government documents on UFO's. The documents give you 10% of the story. But I can see what you mean as well in terms of the cosmic reality that we are relatively aware of."

"Yeah and on our past personal life we at least got the main thing… us, our love for one another."

"What we were doing in the previous life other than being together as a couple? Was I working on Simulation theory in that life? According to your short stories we seemed to be heavily involved in Simulated reality so that means I perhaps was doing the same research as I am now. And what were you doing Lara? On that we are blank."

"Maybe I was living off my beautiful Sarah."

"What about our families? Other friends? Dogs? How did we do for money? What killed us? And hell, what were our second names?"

"We know more about the afterlife."

"Well yeah, if just floating in nothingness and then zap, finding ourselves in a womb is the be-all-and-all."

"But it isn't quite like that is it. The UFO's starting point is the Void. And if you can journey with them then clearly you are not in a womb while that is happening. It implies that the Void isn't just a momentary experience."

"The Mind boggles. I feel a need to know. I am obsessed. I want the whole narrative. I have two first names: Jenny and Sarah. But only one second name that I know of: Quinn".

Sarah parks the car back at her home and the two women exit. Sarah says to Lara

"Come here."

Lara approaches and Sarah kisses her on the lips. She's doing this because she is in love with her and because she wants to remember something else about their past life. And something does surface to consciousness. She suddenly stops kissing Lara and shouts out

"On the bed… at the Lakeside cottage that you were writing about. Crazy guy."

Lara's heart is beating fast. It sounds familiar but is that just because she wrote such similar fiction. Then Lara suddenly feels a rush of excitement and shock race through her body. She can feel it physically as she shouts out "MIKE!!!!!!!!!!!!"

Sarah feels her body go stone cold as the shock of remembering blasts into her conscious mind.

"Mike! F*****g hell, yes, Mike! You schemed to win me from Mike." Sarah pauses for a split second and then continues… "You won and he went crazy!!!"

Lara's heart beats fast. It's like she has just participated in the 100 meter sprint race and she's tired out… "I can't… I can't… I can't believe it. This is impossible." She gets some breath back and desperately asks… "How are we doing this??? I mean, errmmm…. how are we…. remembering this?"

Sarah doesn't respond. She faints instead.

So it was a good night in the end for Sarah and Lara. Except now they think that Lara's scheming was all about winning Sarah's love. But that was only part of it. Both women think there may of been more to Lara's scheming than just winning Sarah's love but the effort is exhausting… and they feel a need to consolidate and bank what they have got. Hence, the Lara that we know that convinced the world of time traveling simulators is still unknown to the two lovers.

The two women go inside. Sarah recovers from her fainting episode. They drink wine while nostalgically listening to songs from the 2030s. Lara gets tipsy and alittle light headed and plays the Corrs song that Sarah put on in their first date in this life… Lara sings along to some of it as she can see the lyrics in the augmented reality version of the song.

"I wonder should I tell you about all the crazy things that I have done?"

"I was searching for an answer in a world so full of strangers. But what I found was never really enough. Now that I've found you, I'm looking in the eyes of love."

Lara is singing these words with her face milimeters away from Sarah's. She continues to sing…

"Please believe me when I say, this time I won't runaway… I swear by all the heavens stars above! Now that I've found you, I'm looking in the eyes of love."

"I can see you and me walking in this world together. Oh my heart's found a home… I've been dreaming of… Now that I've found you, I'm looking in the eyes of love."

Sarah bursts into tears of love and happiness and they hug like they did just days ago when they discovered each other on the train.

Sarah and Lara have been in-love many times across the timelines but never quite as much as on this timeline. On this timeline it feels extra special. The tears flow and they are all about love.

"Never leave me Lara."

"Never."

Sarah walks out the room but not for wine for once. Its for tissues.

"We are out of tissues. I will put them on the shopping list…. I'm joking. I've got them here."

"My scheming in my past life was well worth it" Lara says wiping tears from her eyes.

When the tears had dried they got to speculating about any other scheming Lara could have been involved in. But they got absolutely nowhere near to the correct answer. Sarah was far too in love to think of anything at all negative about Lara. Its one thing to think that you got up to some crazy things… but its another level multiplied by a million to think about one's lover telling a cosmic lie to the entire world's population. Sarah was never going to go there in a million light years. Then just as the tears had dried they started up again when Sarah got down on one knee and said

"Lara. Will you marry me?"

"Yes. A billion times YES!!!"

4. Tragedy

Sarah and Lara had both gone out to tell their friends and family their great news. They were so excited to tell everyone they know that they agreed that they would do it individually as they wanted to spread the word as fast as possible. They could have done it together technologically but people still liked the very old fashioned way of receiving this news…. face to face. Except to say, that almost everyone asked "Well, where is she?"

Jenny entered the relevant part of the City University of New York (CUNY) and waited outside a lecture hall where her best friend, Amy Barker works as a lecturer in Philosophy. Amy has similar interests in the nature of reality to Jenny which helps them get on well. With the lecture over Jenny walked into the lecture hall.

"You do realise that people who are not employed by the University nor a student are not even supposed to be in the University Jenny?" said Amy slightly laughing. She didn't really care given that its Jenny.

Jenny is just about to respond when she remembers an Amy from her previous life that was also her best friend. The memory of such a significant person on one's life that had been forgotten shocks Jenny to the core. She could have fainted right then and there on the spot. But she partially composed herself.

"Well I just pretend to be a tutor. I have done work at other NYC Universities and flash some ID from there and people let me go where I want. But man this University is huge."

"Yup. 243,000 students!"

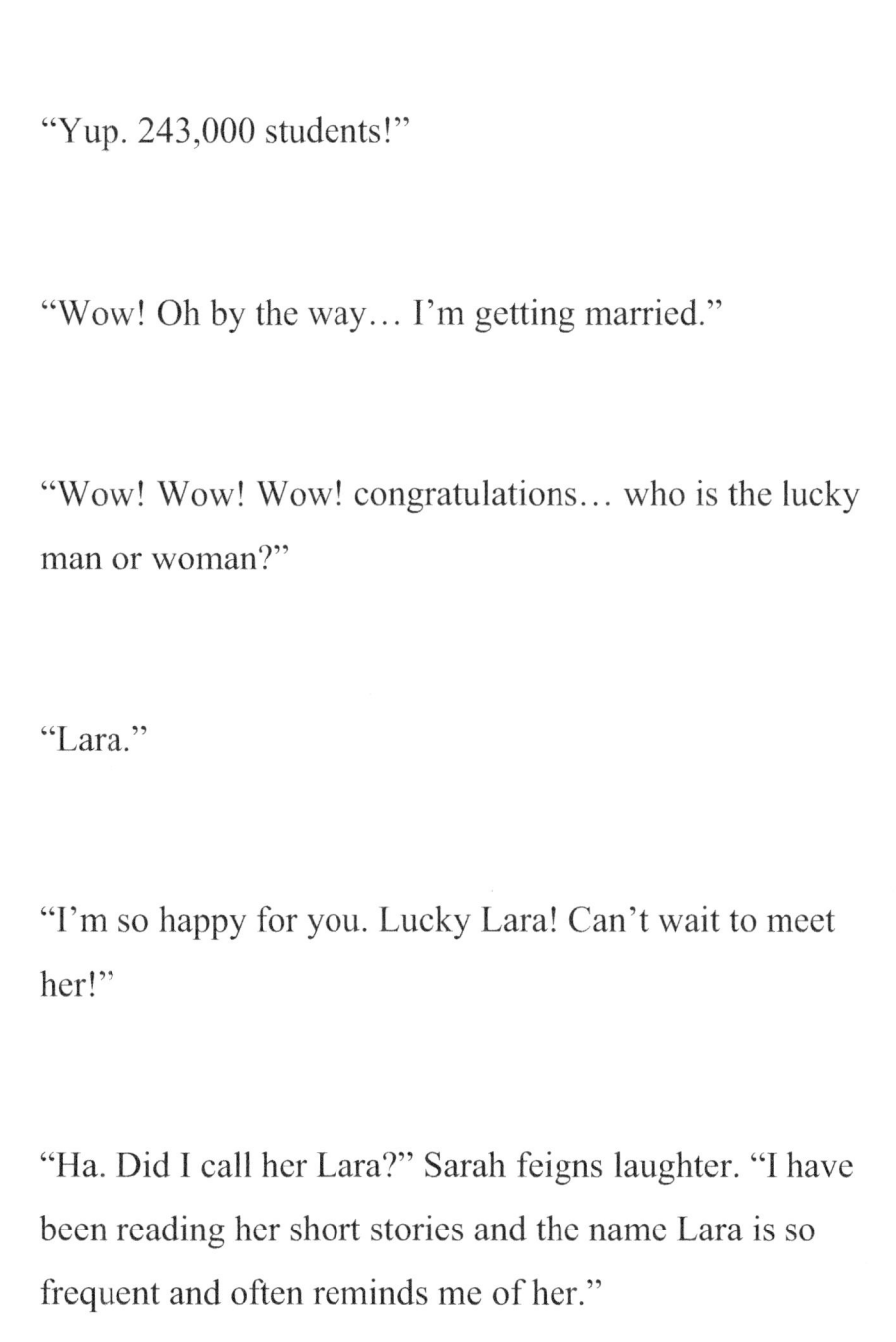

"Wow! Oh by the way… I'm getting married."

"Wow! Wow! Wow! congratulations… who is the lucky man or woman?"

"Lara."

"I'm so happy for you. Lucky Lara! Can't wait to meet her!"

"Ha. Did I call her Lara?" Sarah feigns laughter. "I have been reading her short stories and the name Lara is so frequent and often reminds me of her."

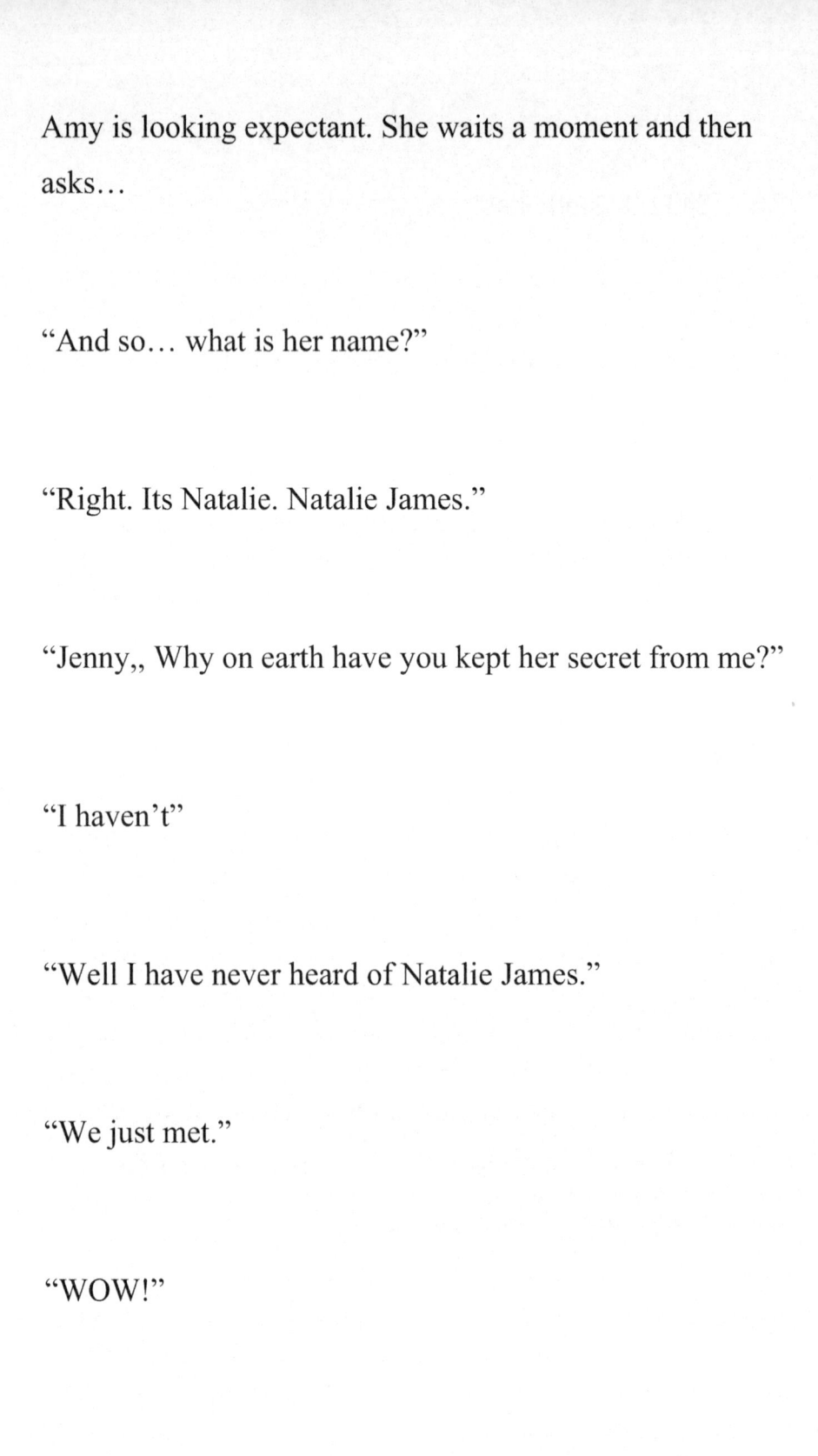

Amy is looking expectant. She waits a moment and then asks…

"And so… what is her name?"

"Right. Its Natalie. Natalie James."

"Jenny,, Why on earth have you kept her secret from me?"

"I haven't"

"Well I have never heard of Natalie James."

"We just met."

"WOW!"

"Amy, I'm going to ask for one thing here. I ask for your full support despite what I just said."

Amy looks at Sarah full in the eyes. She knows that this woman is smart. She's not an idiot teenager. She knows Sarah (or Jenny in Amy's mind) is not the mental age of a teenager. She's mature. But she is confused because this isn't the sort of thing she would do. She continues to look at Sarah.

"Well, Amy?…"

"Ermm, yes, Yes! Of course I support you. I am just gobsmacked that's all. But yes, if anyone gives you grief over it then you can rely on me to support you."

"Thank you Amy. I still have to tell my parents."

"Hey, how about a double date? You and Natalie… me and Pete? Sycamore Wine Bar, 8pm tonight?"

"Deal, unless Natalie isn't up for it. We will be there unless I phone you back in the next half hour saying otherwise."

"Ok c ya later then. I can't wait to meet Natalie."

"C ya."

Lara is up for it. She can't wait. So keen are they that they arrive at Sycamore a-little early. Amy and Pete arrive bang on time. Pete is a vet and has his vets bag with him. That is a conversational starter.

"Is that your vets bag?" asks Jenny.

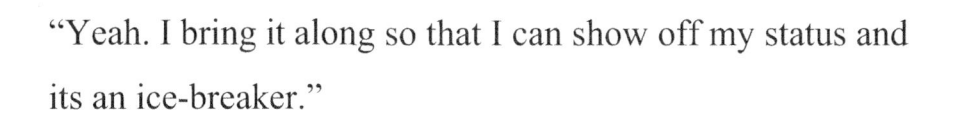

"Yeah. I bring it along so that I can show off my status and its an ice-breaker."

"Really?" asks a slightly nervous Natalie who just wants to get in on the conversation.

"Hhmmm, not really. Its in-case of emergencies."

"Come on then, lets order the drinks" says Jenny.

The couples settle down to a night of getting merry downing wines. And after about 40 minutes Pete notices his nephew (Adam) and his mate (Jim) enter the bar.

"So what's in a vets bag Pete?" asks Natalie again trying extra hard to be conversational.

Pete picks the bag up and opens it. "Nothing exciting" he says. He drops it back to the ground quickly as a friend of Amy's and Jenny's walks over to say hi. She just makes some small talk and then is on her way. Pete hasn't zipped the bag back up.

Meanwhile Adam points out to Jim that's his uncle.

Jim says "Let's have some fun tonight."

"What have you got in mind?"

"I dunno yet. Let me think" replies Jim.

"Actually, I know" says Adam observing his Uncles open vets bag. He continues "You see that bag that my Uncle has got? Well that's his vets bag."

"And?"

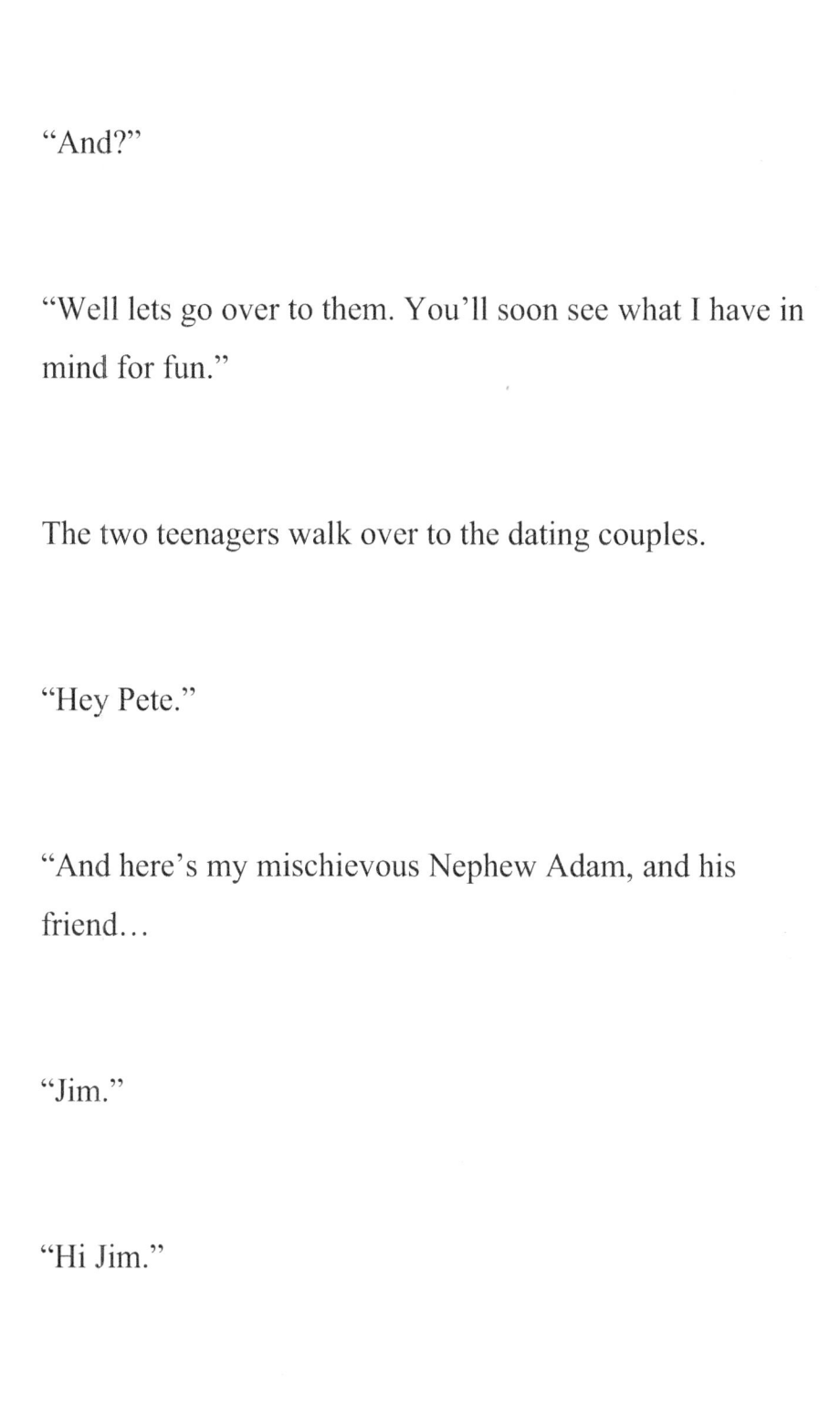

"Well lets go over to them. You'll soon see what I have in mind for fun."

The two teenagers walk over to the dating couples.

"Hey Pete."

"And here's my mischievous Nephew Adam, and his friend…

"Jim."

"Hi Jim."

"Just thought I would be nosy and see what's going on over here" says Adam.

"Well these two are getting married and we are dating. And hey, you two are under 21 so whats going on here? I tell you what though, we would like this to be a double date, not a double date plus baby sitting, so I would like to offer to buy you two a couple of illegal drinks that you can drink in peace away from us?"

"Thanks, Budweiser please."

"Make that two" says Jim.

"Anyone else ready for another?"

Jenny puts her hand in the air.

Pete goes to the bar. And at that very second Adam's cell phone buzzes as he has a text message. He takes his cell out of his pocket then pretends to carelessly drop it. In reality he has deliberately dropped it into his Uncles vets bag. He picks his cell back up along with a sealed bag of Ketamine. He carefully, without anyone noticing, places the Ketamine in his pocket.

Pete is ordering the drinks. He also orders one for himself, when he shouts over to Amy… "Amy, can you bring these drinks to the table, I have to go to the men's room."

Adam shouts over "I can do that." As he does so he sneakily pours a generous quantity of liquid form ketamine into Jenny's drink.

He takes the drinks over to the table.

The teens act polite and then sit a fair distance away from the two couples but close enough to still able to keep an eye on them. Adam and Jim's attitude is very naive. They are thinking that they have merely played a prank on their Uncles friend. The problem is that Adam had administered an excessive ketamine overdose and Jenny is soon feeling very ill.

Jenny slurs her words, "I can't see properly, there's something wrong… with my hearing." These words are not really audible to the others, and when she tries to stand up she loses consciousness and collapses back down on the table.

"SARAH!" screams out Lara much to everyone else's momentary confusion. But they have an emergency to deal with and thus are not going to start questioning Natalie on getting Jenny's name wrong. Natalie is trying to wake Jenny.

"Call 911" orders Natalie.

The two teenagers are looking on from a distance with a disturbed look on their faces. They are already regretting what they have done.

Pete has dialed 911 and emergency services are on their way.

"Nooo, No. Don't leave me" Lara is saying with tears again streaming down her face. Amy, standing behind Lara has her hands on her face, shocked at what has just happened and what she is witnessing. Lara is pleading with Sarah to wake up and each time she does so she uses the name Sarah.

Emergency services arrive. They declare Sarah dead on the scene. On hearing the emergency service personnel confirm this to one another Lara screams out in pain

"NOOOOOOOOO!" She breaks down on the spot as Amy tries her best to console her. But there is no consoling her. She is crying her eyes out as the cruel turn of events is impossible for Lara to take. She refuses any help from anyone. She takes Sarah's keys and goes back to the house. Amy and Pete could do nothing to stop her. And of course, they don't even know Lara.

Back at Sarah's house Lara contemplates committing suicide in order to be with Sarah in the Void. But she feared reincarnating and losing all connection to Sarah. Back in the Void Sarah is desperate to contact Lara. Sarah now has full knowledge of all of her history with Lara. But she isn't happy. She is not happy at all that she lost her life. But her concern is about Lara. She wants her to be happy. And she is suffering badly for Lara, she is hating seeing her like this. And she is seeing her like this as Sarah has transferred her consciousness to Lara. But much to Sarah's despair Lara is unable to sense her presence. Lara is crying out for Sarah and Sarah is right there. But Lara does not know that Sarah is right there. Lara drinks herself to sleep and does not get up at all the next day. She spends all day feeling physically sick and mentally wrecked. Her family and a friend think she is getting married. They have no idea of Sarah's address. Hence she is not disturbed by them knocking on the door. She does receive phone calls but she ignores them completely. In the rare occasions she thinks of anything, it is suicide that she thinks about. The day after is similar. There was only one slight difference. This time she does ignore door knocks from Pete and Amy. And when she thinks about suicide she thinks about UFOs and journeying with them across time and space. This is not some adventure minded consideration in Lara's mind. She is interested in that part of the nature of reality because it means that reincarnation can't possibly be all that happened to her and Sarah in the Void. It sounds like the Void is a place where you can exist for some time. She plays back in her mind Sarah saying "We went to them as opposed to them abducting us [and their starting point was] the Void." Lara gets up out of bed the following day. Her mind-state isn't even considering what killed Sarah. Because although initially devastated she is recovering fast due to her view that she knows that there is no death.

Consciousness continues on in the Void. She is now determined to kill herself to free her consciousness from this earthly realm. Her family would be left a very lengthy note informing them that she is not really dead. Lara wondered how this would come across to them? Simulation theory had been largely accepted which implies simulators. However, people killing themselves is still as big a no no as it always has been. But Lara's decisiveness is well over 50%. She thinks that the only thing that would stop her from taking her own (earthly) life would be if Sarah somehow returned. Lara doesn't think a ghostly Sarah returning would be enough. But what is the Void like in terms of materialization? Lara hadn't cracked the entire cosmic puzzle and those gaps were keeping her decisiveness below 100%.

That night as she slept she heard a voice in her dreams. It was Sarah. She was dreaming of Sarah going online on a site called 'Any life' and saying a password of 'Brooklyn 3756'. The voice said to her "Join me Lara. I have proven that this really is me." Lara's eyes popped open and she logged into 'Any Life' by stating Sarah's account password. Lara shouts out-loud

"YAAASSSS!!!!! YESSSS!!! YESSSS!!!" The joy that impacted Lara's mind and body was immense. Indescribable.

"Thank you! Thank you! Thank you! Thank you!"

Sarah's consciousness is right there viewing her account page with Lara and viewing Lara's reaction. Lara is convinced Sarah is right there with her so she says…

"Sarah… Hold me, kiss me." Sarah is consciousness so cannot physically do that BUT she has a sense of movement and is right there sharing the same space as Lara. But its not enough for Lara to know that Sarah is there. She wants to experience Sarah as being with her. Hence…

…The only question now is… not will Lara commit suicide. Rather it's… how will Lara commit suicide?

Lara paces back and forth in Sarah's front room. She says out-loud…

"Train. How we met on this timeline. How it will end on this timeline."

Sarah's reaction is along the lines of "What a coincidence" because she is now aware of a past simulated experience of Lara and Sarah being hit by a train in Boston Station and then suddenly finding themselves in the Void. She wishes she could calm Lara who Sarah views as being frantic. Nevertheless only a week ago the thought of dying was terrifying for Sarah, hence she understands Lara's reaction easily enough…. it's just that Sarah now knows it is not the end at all. So the fear is unnecessary. However, Lara is stalling.

That night Lara is still very much alive having not gone through with the suicide. In her dreams Sarah tells Lara to play Runaway by the Corrs and to listen to the lyrics and to watch the video. She hears Sarah singing the song in her dream. On awaking Lara knows she had never heard this song before until hearing Sarah singing it in her dreams. So she plays it in waking life. And it is identical to how she heard it in her sleep. Of course, Sarah had chosen a love song. And when Lara watched the accompanying video to the song, she observes the train journey and train stations.

https://www.youtube.com/watch?v=0fMUYU8DC1U

"WOW!!!" said Lara out-loud.

This brings tears of joy to Lara once again. And now she is set to do something that few humans have done before. She is going to commit suicide in a mind-state of joy, not depression. She gets dressed at lightening speed and heads for Grand Central Station. Seconds after exiting Sarah's house she sees a Police Car pull up outside. She has no doubt it is in relation to Sarah's death but she is not interested. The police did not see Lara leave the home so she lets them waste their time. Lara has only one thing on her mind and she will stop for no-one.

Once in Grand Central Station she waits for a works train that is just passing through. And to the absolute horror of multiple witnesses, some of whom were screaming, Lara, without hesitation, threw herself right in-front of the train. She is killed instantly on impact.

Within about 2 seconds Lara hears Sarah's voice saying "You did it Lara. I love you."

Lara responds quoting Runaway… "I'm never gonna stop falling in love with you."

5. Cosmic Connection

A mere few days of Lara's life had been viewed by her as far more significant than all her previous 33 years and this is because Lara was well aware that with Sarah she had a far larger cosmic connection. She had been aware of that fact within seconds of having met on the train. The impact of that meeting on Sarah's and Lara's family members and closest friends is devastating and seriously harms over ten people's mental health. Pete and Amy are questioned a-lot but they are as confused as anyone, especially about the times one or both of them refer to the wrong names. The coincidence of both Jenny and Natalie referring to wrong name frustrates Pete and Amy… especially when Natalie was begging Jenny to not leave her because that begging as her lover was dying was not exactly a time when you would use a different name for someone... its a time when you would be at your most serious. Surely?

Pete's nephew received prison time for murder and this put a huge strain on his and Amy's relationship which collapsed within weeks. While Sarah and Lara could be accused of not thinking of others their experience of the nature of reality is unique as they were able to recall so much about the nature of reality and their personal connection to one another. Whereas 99.9999999999% of the human species has 100% amnesia about anything prior to this life. Nevertheless Sarah and Lara did transfer their consciousness to the two funerals. And while this did not make them regret Lara deliberately taking her own life, it did make them feel some guilt. But even that guilt was soon dismissed, replaced by blaming Adam for administering Jenny's drink with a killer drug. Sarah and Lara tried to help the bereaved family members, and a few close friends, that were deeply hurt and confused, but not one single one of those close one's could sense their presence. It was deeply frustrating for Sarah and Lara who had hoped that they could communicate to earth bound consciousness in its sleep. After-all it had worked when Sarah communicated to Lara that way. But it was no use. Hardly anyone it seems, can sense a ghosts presence. This is something that Sarah and Lara dislike about the nature of reality. And Jenny became especially frustrated by her inability to make contact with earth bound consciousness when Amy, already in mourning for the loss of her best friend, and having broken up with her boyfriend, was 8 days later diagnosed with breast cancer and informed she had less than 2 years to live. Jenny tried everything to make contact with her, frequently transferring her consciousness to such a spot that meant that Amy would have to walk right through her. But it had no more impact on Amy than someone shouting her name on Planet Pluto would have. It saddened Jenny that she was actually longing for those 2 years to pass for Amy so that she could be liberated from all of her misery. Sarah and Lara were now aware that even when Void bound consciousness used UFO's (that can bridge earth time/space and the void) that even in abduction the earth consciousness and void consciousness do not materialize for one another and communication is distorted.

"I don't think you can do anything for Amy" said Lara.

"We know what it is like to be an earthbound human being. Its so wrong that we know what they are going through but are blocked from helping them. I mean how cruel is that??!!"

"What about if you go to a far in the distant future earth bound realm… making sure that it is the same time-line as the Amy that you are concerned about. Then in this future earthbound realm they will have tracked consciousness into the afterlife. You then communicate with someone from that earthbound timeline, asking them to travel back in time and communicate a message to Amy."

Sarah thought that sounded highly convoluted but responded with…

"Well, what the timeline we just visited needs is a time-traveler from the distant future to travel back in time and provide them with the technology that connects earthbound consciousness to afterlife void consciousness."

Lara responded… "Ahh, I see. We would be able to contact the future earth-bound consciousness as they possess the technology to communicate with the Void consciousness. Thus they probably provide that tech to countless timelines and parallel universes. The timelines we are aware of just haven't been given the candy yet."

"Correct… and not surprising given that there could be an infinite number of timelines once you grasp the implications of all these timelines branching out."

So Sarah and Lara searched for a universe and a timeline in which this technology had been discovered. That is a profoundly innovative technology, of cosmic historical significance that connects earthbound and Void consciousness. But each time they thought they were getting close they discovered that something would happen that prevented the technological breakthrough from being unleashed. Most often the event that would prevent the unleashing of the technology was a war that kept sending humanity back to the Middle Ages. Sarah's and Lara's concern level, and frustration level, motivated them up to a point. But they had each other so they did not seek until they find. They tried… they worked hard but this wasn't a case of giving 100%. They gave up before that point.

Sarah and Lara bemoaned the lack of ability to connect the two worlds but hoped that UFO's would propel humanity to understanding that the two worlds are connected. At the back of their minds they understood that they hadn't ever been on a universes timeline that was strong on UFOs as bridges between earth life and the afterlife. So this was more frustration albeit that specific frustration equated to back of the mind frustration. What was more front and center was that the timeline they had just lived in, up until age 33, hadn't even gone through a Lue Elizondo, Chris Mellon, Tom Delonge style Disclosure process. Rather UFO's were still (in their most recent 2056 universes timeline) considered to be akin to belief in fairies and/or super hero comic strip category. It would be an exaggeration to say that Sarah and Lara were devastated by all of this. Again, the correct word is frustrated. They had each other. And they are not saints. Ultimately having each other is what counts for them. Nevertheless their ethical or moral concern for Amy and their families persisted. The two women were hurt enough concerning their awareness that the people they had left behind were living a life of cluelessness about the true nature of reality. And that cluelessness means that Amy and their families were experiencing unnecessary pain and anguish. They were experiencing unnecessary trauma over life and death issues. And yet there is no such thing as death. So when Lara stepped in-front of the train the onlookers screamed at the actions of an irrational insane idiot. When Lara's close-ones discovered what she had done they not only broke down into a mental state of utter despair and heartbreak, they also wondered about Lara's mental breakdown. When did she go crazy? They thought it was on meeting Jenny. And then there is the confusion about calling Jenny by a different name… calling her Sarah. And Jenny called Natalie by a different name… Lara. Was that to do with a mental illness? What is for sure is that when Sarah and Lara transferred their consciousness to that universe and timeline they soon realized that their reputations were ruined. On the one hand they considered that assessment of themselves to be unfair. On the other hand they felt a guilty conscience. Their frustrations grew.

From the Void's cosmic perspective both women were regressing into bitterness. However, to bring us up to the current day (whatever that means!) it is as if the cosmic order or karmic nature of reality agreed with Sarah and Lara as it gave them a chance to put right what once went wrong. Although to say "agreed with Sarah and Lara" might be stretching the truth way too far as they did not want reincarnation. But they were reincarnated back on the timeline they had invested so much frustration over. This meant 33 years of Sarah and Lara not knowing one another. Then in 2056 they met on the train and felt the same cosmic connection across space and time as before. In-fact at this point there are fractional discrepancies from the previous time they were on this timeline. This is due to even greater deja vu between Sarah and Lara. It means that a new almost identical timeline is created. One discrepanency is that they had not got engaged. The Sycamore Wine bar incident still happened with Sarah and Lara every bit as in-love as before but still just girlfriends. They were not engaged and the reason for this is due to their cosmic connection being experienced as a love for one another that goes beyond this earthly existence.

Sarah and Lara can't wait for the double date to start so they arrive at Sycamore wine bar a-little early. Amy and Pete arrive bang on time. Pete is a vet and has his vets bag with him. That is a conversational starter.

"Is that your vets bag?" asks Jenny.

"Yeah. I bring it along so that I can show off my status and its an ice-breaker."

"Really?" asks a slightly nervous Natalie who just wants to get in on the conversation.

"Hhmmm, not really. Its in-case of emergencies."

"Come on then, lets order the drinks" says Jenny.

The couples settle down to a night of getting merry downing wines. And after about 40 minutes Pete notices his nephew (Adam) and his mate (Jim) enter the bar.

"So what's in a vets bag Pete?" asks Natalie again trying extra hard to be conversational.

Pete picks the bag up and opens it. "Nothing exciting" he says. He drops it back to the ground quickly as a friend of Amy's and Jenny's walks over to say hi. She just makes some small talk and then is on her way. Pete hasn't zipped the bag back up.

Meanwhile Adam points out to Jim that's his uncle.

Jim says "Let's have some fun tonight."

"What have you got in mind?"

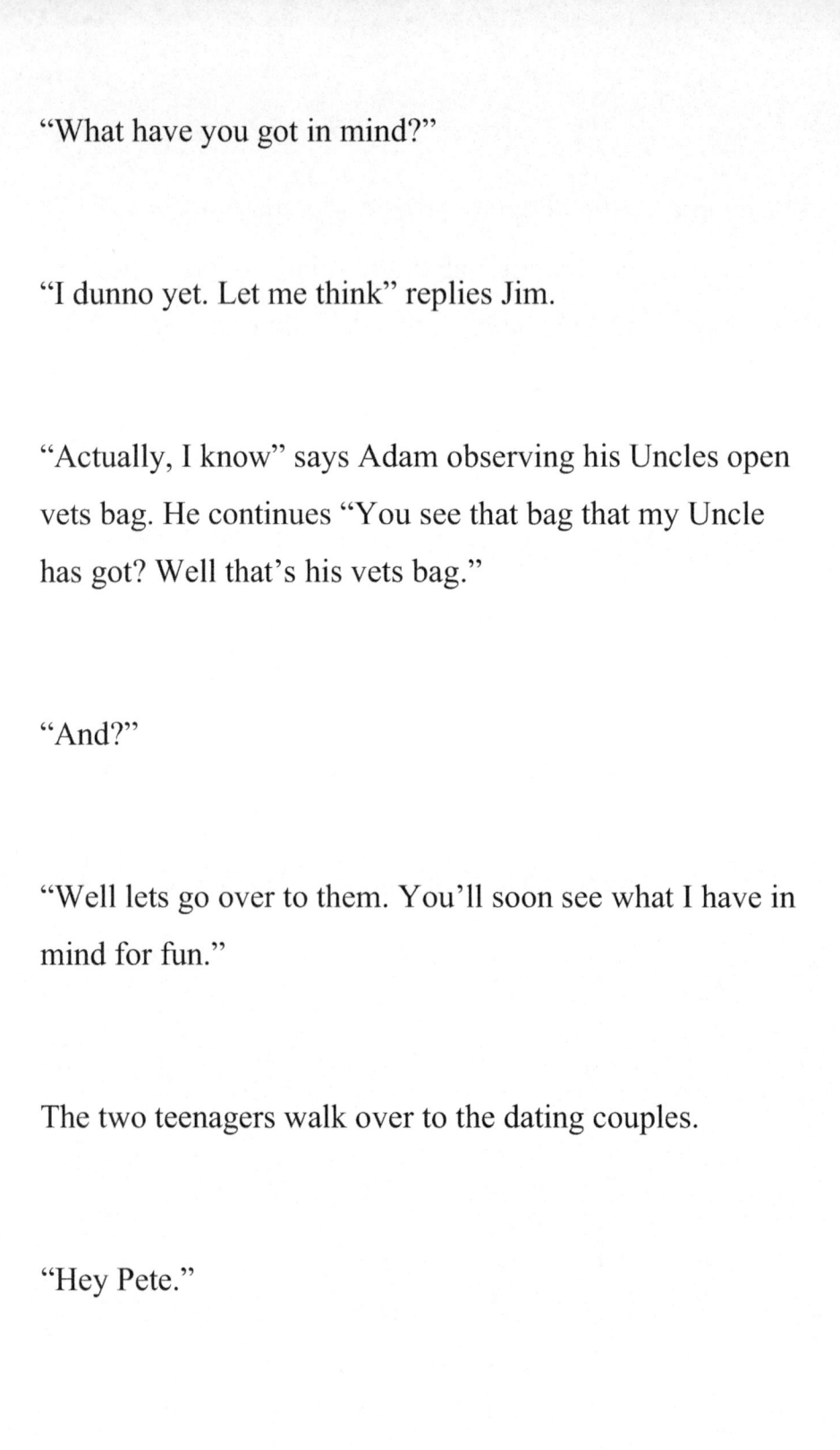

"I dunno yet. Let me think" replies Jim.

"Actually, I know" says Adam observing his Uncles open vets bag. He continues "You see that bag that my Uncle has got? Well that's his vets bag."

"And?"

"Well lets go over to them. You'll soon see what I have in mind for fun."

The two teenagers walk over to the dating couples.

"Hey Pete."

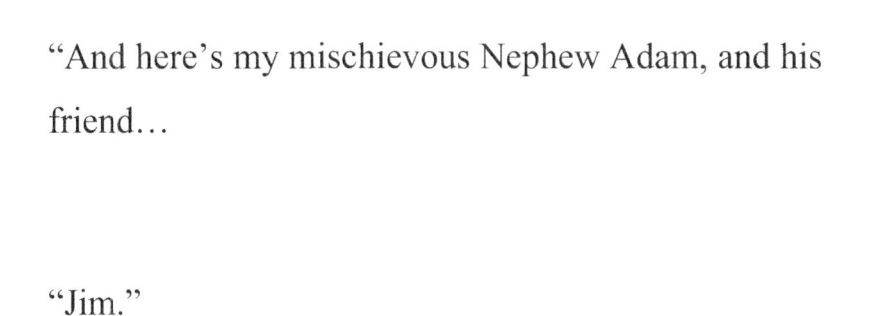

"And here's my mischievous Nephew Adam, and his friend…

"Jim."

"Hi Jim."

"Just thought I would be nosy and see what's going on over here" says Adam.

"Double dating. And hey, you two are under 21 so whats going on here? I tell you what though, we would like this to be a double date, not a double date plus baby sitting, so I would like to offer to buy you two a couple of illegal drinks that you can drink in peace away from us?"

"Thanks, Budweiser please."

"Make that two" says Jim.

"Anyone else ready for another?"

Jenny puts her hand in the air.

Pete goes to the bar. And at that very second Adam's cell phone buzzes as he has a text message. He takes his cell out of his pocket then pretends to carelessly drop it. In reality he has deliberately dropped it into his Uncles vets bag. He picks his cell back up along with a sealed bag of Ketamine. He carefully, without anyone noticing, places the Ketamine in his pocket.

Pete is ordering the drinks. He also orders one for himself, when he shouts over to Amy… "Amy, can you bring these drinks to the table, I have to go to the men's room."

Adam shouts over "I can do that." As he does so he subtely and liberally pours liquid form ketamine into Jenny's drink.

He takes the drinks over to the table.

The teens act polite and then sit a fair distance away from the two couples but still able to keep an eye on them. Adam and Jim's attitude is very naive. They are thinking that they have merely played a prank on their Uncles friend. The problem is that Adam had administered an excessive ketamine overdose.

And then, all of a sudden Lara remembers! She recalls this event happening in her previous life as if it had happened yesterday. She shouts out "SARAH, STOP!" And Lara grabs her drink and moves it out of reach of her lover. Lara then stands up and shouts over to the two teenagers "YOU HAVE DRUGGED SARAH HAVEN'T YOU! I REMEMBER!!!". Total confusion is what Pete and Amy feel with this wrong name phenomenon continuing on and on and on. And then suddenly again, Lara is hit like an atomic bomb going off inside her head. She is suddenly able to recall ALL SEVEN of her previous existences and the Void and the visits to other parallel universes when Lara and Sarah transferred their consciousness. ALL of them, involved Sarah. But this is overwhelming. It is too much. It is draining her energy. It is exhausting. Lara vomits all over the floor. She then starts to slur her words. Pete and Amy are the one's who are attending to Lara. Lara quickly passes into unconsciousness. Sarah screams out "LAARRRRAAA!!!!". Sarah then strangely sits back in her chair. Pete shouts "SOMEONE DIAL 911." Then out of the corner of her eye Amy sees Sarah with vomit beside her. She has threw up as well. Amy neglects Lara to go to her best friends aid. At almost that exact second Sarah collapses into unconsciousness. Sarah had also remembered all her past 7 lives, all with Lara and experienced it as exhausting and overwhelming. As with Lara, Sarah also remembers not only her own previous lives, but also the transferring of her consciousness to other parallel universes when she transferred her consciousness there. She also remembers the simulation when she found herself in the dentists chair. And so on.

Pete shouts out "What the f**k is in that drink?"

Amy replies "No one touched that drink!"

Both women are rushed to hospital but the doctors and nurses tests indicate nothing other than perfect physical health. They say that they agree with Sarah and Lara that it is exhaustion. That being said, the medical professionals are for sure, shocked that they both went down synchronistically. The doctors and nurses are a tad irritated by Pete and Amy's talk of that being impossible and of their constant references to Jenny and Natalie calling each other Sarah and Lara.

"None of it makes sense" says Amy to one of the doctors.

The next day Sarah enters Lara's hospital room.

"Hi you."

"Hi Sarah."

Sarah smiles very widely and says "Its Psy-Op Lara, my Apocalypse lover!"

Lara smiles even wider and in a highly sarcastic tone of voice says "I'm saying nothing. You are really strong with a wine bottle when you smash it over a human beings skull."

"Yayyyy! Saved your life. But take some credit Lara… you actually penned it in your book called 'Stalker'. You write about Sarah saving Lara's life from a crazy guy. She saves her life by smashing him over the head and killing him with a wine bottle. Exactly like happened in real life."

"How many times have we called each other Sarah and Lara in the company of Amy and Pete? They must think we are bonkers!"

But Sarah and Lara are not bonkers. They are the first ever people that have ever lived that have remembered all of their previous existences. They are special.

Sarah says "We are living in a society that knows nothing. We are outcasts in such a society. If we told the truth we would be told we are crazy for the rest of our lives. People would wonder what on earth has gone wrong with us."

"I don't hate them. I don't even dislike them. We can recall our concern for Amy in the previous incarnation here and our families. And yet…

"go on."

"And yet we can't live with them."

"You liberate me from this narrow prison. Everyone in this world is cosmically unconscious. We know everything. They know absolutely nothing." Sarah continues… "My career feels meaningless now. I do not have any questions or theories. I already know the answers. My career feels like it belongs in a previous century."

"Yeah, I don't want to pretend that we are the same as everyone else and yet I do not want to be told I am crazy. I think Sarah, that we have to pack our bags and isolate ourselves from the rest of civilization. We cannot prove what we are saying unless we murder people. And we aren't going to do that."

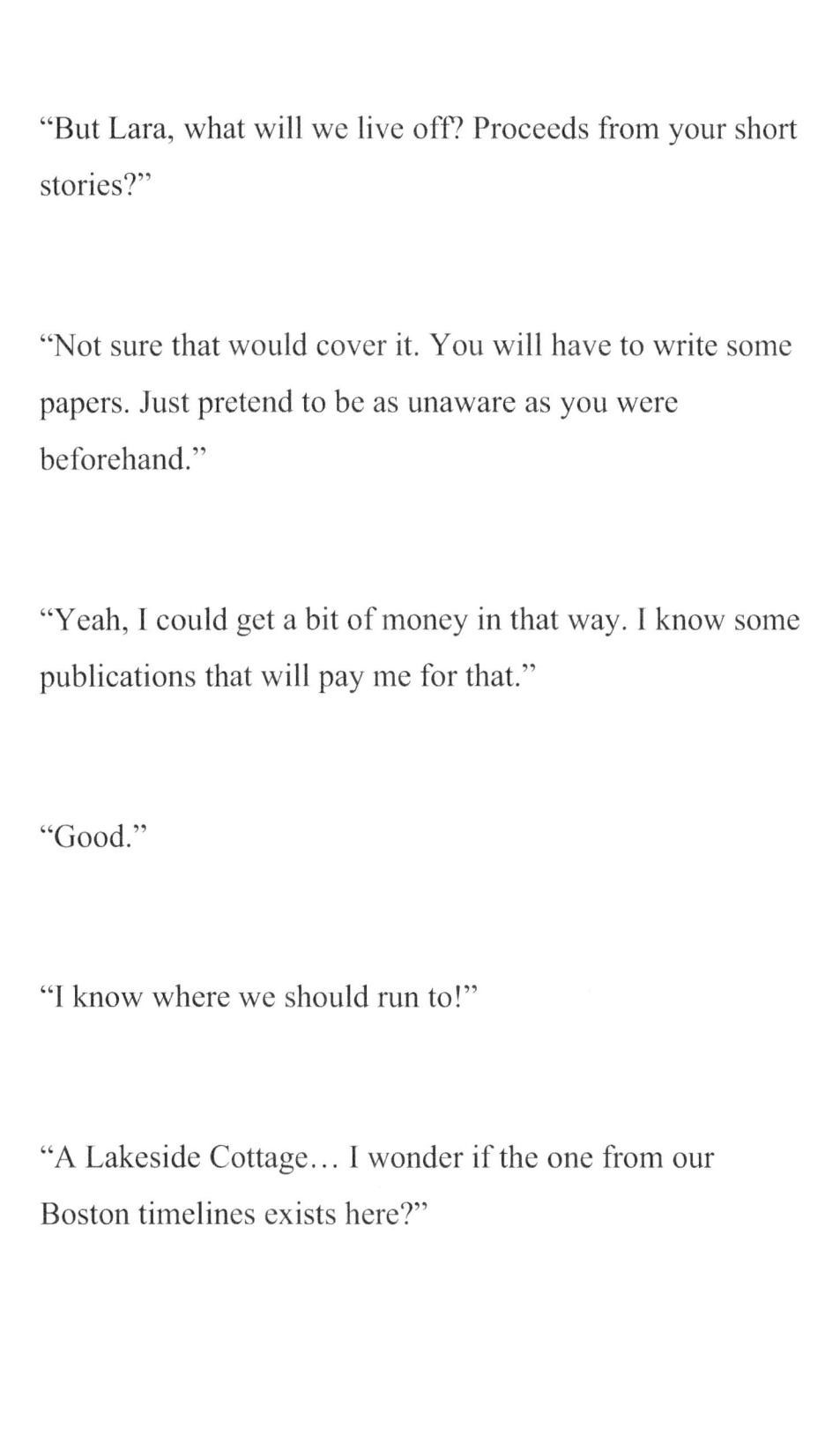

"But Lara, what will we live off? Proceeds from your short stories?"

"Not sure that would cover it. You will have to write some papers. Just pretend to be as unaware as you were beforehand."

"Yeah, I could get a bit of money in that way. I know some publications that will pay me for that."

"Good."

"I know where we should run to!"

"A Lakeside Cottage… I wonder if the one from our Boston timelines exists here?"

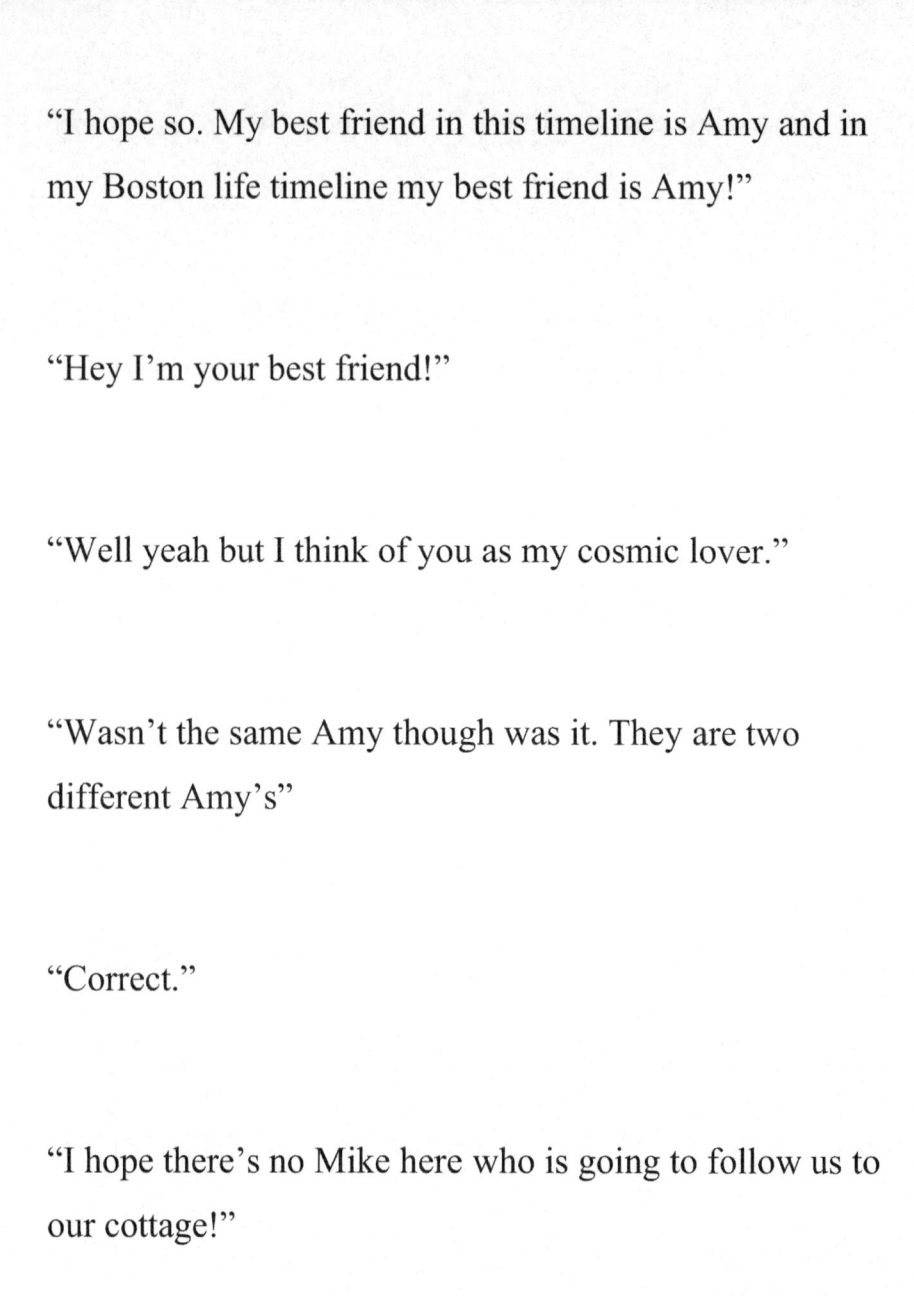

"I hope so. My best friend in this timeline is Amy and in my Boston life timeline my best friend is Amy!"

"Hey I'm your best friend!"

"Well yeah but I think of you as my cosmic lover."

"Wasn't the same Amy though was it. They are two different Amy's"

"Correct."

"I hope there's no Mike here who is going to follow us to our cottage!"

"Ha. Are you sure you don't want that. We found him to be hilarious entertainment under that bed hiding while we flirted with one another and stripped off and made love."

"Not at the time we didn't. It was only hilarious watching on as ghosts!"

"Ghosts! I hate that word. We are consciousness. We transfer our consciousness."

Suddenly Amy came in.

"Hi Sarah and Lara. Nice chat you are having. I've been listening to it from the very start. And I recorded most of it because it was sounding so good. It sounded intriguing from the get-go. So Jenny… I mean Sarah, who is Amy from your Boston timeline? And why can't you two prove anything unless you murder people with a bottle of wine? And how do you spectate events as ghosts when neither of you are dead?" And when did you go mad Jenny slash Sarah? You seemed sane a week ago."

"Sorry to disappoint you Amy. But I am a short story writer. Our chat was fiction. That is how I get ideas. We work well, as a team."

Amy doesn't believe them and is a little irritated that she thinks she has just been lied to. She responds

"So Jenny slash Sarah… is that why you screamed out the name LARA when you saw your lover collapse last night?"

"Yeah, she uses that name so much that its her nickname in my mind."

Amy scoffs. She's thinking she's being fed cover story bullshit. But she also thinks they have covered up quite effectively.

Amy turns her attention back to Lara.

"Natalie slash Lara… last night you accused Pete's nephew and his mate of spiking Jenny's drink. In that moment, when you surely weren't thinking of short-stories, you called Jenny… Sarah. May I ask why?"

"Nickname. She calls me Lara. So I respond by calling her Sarah."

"Oh come one!!! So, you two won't be running off to a Boston cottage then?"

"Nah. Boston is a city. There's no lakeside cottage…."

Amy interrupts …. "I'm aware you were referring to outskirts. I'm not stupid! So when you are chatting about your short stories you refer to being a short story writer in the story saying you will live off your short story earnings… rather confusing the reader don't you think? And you even made a comparison between what Natalie penned in her book called Stalker and a real life event."

Sarah responds "She's got a good point Natalie. You should stop doing those things."

Lara nods in agreement. Amy laughs.

Sarah argues the point… "Hey we were talking about ghosts at a cottage. Of course we were talking in terms of fiction. Think about it Amy."

"It appears that I am going to be in your next short story Lara… I mean Natalie. Or is it Lara? You hardly know me. So isn't that a tad odd that you want to write about me? I would call it creepy."

Lara nods again. Sarah says "She's got a point." Amy laughs again and says "So you remember your concern for me from your previous incarnation here. I seem like I might have been quite central to the storyline. You also say we will think you are both crazy. I find it strange that you both had such a bad night last night and yet with no hesitation right from the off you are discussing short story plans, not real life synchronicitically both collapsing… and you both know that's what you are doing and neither wants to talk about last nights real event. But of course neither of you were discussing fiction were you? Not that I think either of you are in-touch with reality. You are both crazy."

Sarah starts to argue back…

"Look Amy. You heard me refer to you as best friend. That was true. I care about you. You do not need to know anything else. You are a good person. We are good people. Now please leave us alone. Lara means you no harm. And Amy… get yourself checked out for breast cancer."

"What?????"

"I'm being serious. IF you get yourself checked out for Breast cancer then I will tell you the truth. Deal? Look you have good health insurance, you are living in New York City. There's medical professionals all over the city specializing in breast cancer screening and diagnosis. You can definitely access an immediate screening. So if you want the truth do that for me and for yourself please."

Amy rolls her eyes but doesn't think Jenny is a bad person. She just doesn't know whats going on and would like to know. She walks out as she doesn't think its worth falling out with Jenny over this. However she is planning on following them when they are allowed to leave the hospital because as she listened to the recording of the bizarre dialogue between Sarah and Lara, her main takeaway from it was that Sarah planned to disown her. It was this bit of the recording that Amy thought a little hurtful:

"I don't hate them. I don't even dislike them. We can recall our concern for Amy in the previous incarnation here and our families. And yet…"

"go on."

"And yet we can't live with them."

Amy also thought to herself… so Jenny is disowning me despite thinking I have got breast cancer. That makes no sense.

Sarah and Lara got home… Lara now loved the Corrs. She's looking into Sarah's eyes while singing

"Oh my hearts found a home… I've been dreaming of… Now that I've found you… I'm looking in the eyes of love."

Sarah sings Runaway back at her…

"Say its true, there's nothing like me and you. I'm not alone. Tell me you feel it to…"

"Close the door… lay down upon the floor… and by candlelight make love to me through the night…"

Then Lara says…

"How did it feel to you, Sarah, when it suddenly hit you at Sycamore Wine Bar that you could remember all of your previous existences?"

"So overwhelming, yet beyond words exciting and too much, I wanted to think it all in one go… just grasp it all. And the excitement. And the shock. The shock was too much. So I threw up. Clearly it was the same for you?"

"Absolutely. The shock is enough when its one thing like remembering Mike or remembering the ketamine. But remembering everything like scheming with the CIA, meeting other timeline Sarah and Lara's, getting reincarnated, reliving the same life, fooling the entire world into believing in time travelers who are also our simulators, the apocalypse…"

"So ironic that simulating and time traveling and greys are all real anyway. So much of what happened on one of our timelines was on the one hand bullshit psy-op stuff occurring within a fake Disclosure world… and yet the truth is that UFO's connect this earthly world and the Void. Its a miracle."

"We know more than anyone else that has ever lived and yet Mike could have transferred his consciousness here and we wouldn't even know it. The next time we are showering he will be there in-between us."

Lara laughed her head off at that thought and said "That's more of a problem for him than us as he would be gagging to materialize… ha ha ha. When you think about it there must be consciousnesses all over the place."

"Although there is an infinite or seemingly infinite number of timelines to choose from."

"Yeah, but almost everyone will visit the one they were on in their earthly life."

"Pervs everywhere"

"Ha ha ha ha"… Lara clearly found a hefty amount of the nature of reality quite funny… she found the thought of ubiqutous pervs hilarious.

"No point shutting the drapes" said Lara laughing as she said it. And then she brings up the simulated event when she set Mike up so that he ended up stood in Sarah's shower (behind the curtains)… with Sarah naked about to enter the shower, not knowing that anyone else was in her house. Lara wanted to destroy his reputation in Sarah's mind. In the current moment Lara laughs out loud again, as she recalls that incident.

"You did some crazzzzyyyy things!" replies Sarah.

Amy sat in her car outside the house is hearing all of this as she has a key to Sarah's house and bugged it before Sarah and Lara got back home. She has also bugged Sarah's car. Amy observes that Lara again referred to Sarah instead of Jenny. They seem to think they are God-like... what the f**k! The comment of "We know more than anyone that has ever lived" struck Amy as the most grandiose, inflated and egotistical statement in history. When they started chatting about pervs and Mike the conversation sounded so insane that Amy involuntarily laughed. Suddenly Amy gets a phonecall.

"Hi Pete"

"Amy you won't believe it."

"What?"

"Well you know that Natalie said that it was ketamine?"

"Yeah, she said that."

"The lab results are back… and she's right."

Amy was stunned. "Ok."

But still that doesn't mean all this other cosmic crackerjack stuff has an ounce of validity. She continued to listen to the bugged conversation and was struck by Sarah's upset tone that Amy was going to die because she would never believe us. She heard Lara console her as Sarah cried.

A tear fell from Amy's eye. The lab result and that bit of the otherwise insane conversation meant that she decisively decided to get herself checked out. But she kept listening to the mentally insane conversation and made a note of the address of a lakeside cottage that Sarah had booked for them. Indeed, they were going in 2 days. But first the Breast cancer check.

Amy's check came back negative for cancer. It was a not so subtle difference on this timeline that had the occasional difference from the near identical one that Sarah and Lara had experienced. This made Amy think that Natalie must have seen the ketamine being inserted into Sarah's drink and she must have seen Pete's nephew take it from the vets bag. She had to have seen the label. Amy isn't thinking that Natalie wanted Jenny dead. She's thinking that Natalie is a grandiose nutjob and she's somehow turned Jenny into one too. She wanted the old Jenny back and would stop at nothing to bring her back from Alice in Wonderland existence back to the land of the rational. She felt sorry for Jenny. She now hated Natalie.

6. Amy

Sarah and Lara set off in Sarah's car to their new holiday home. They are blasting out and singing along to Closer by the Corrs.

"What does it mean, what will I see, if I look closer…"

https://www.youtube.com/watch?v=Q7ldkWYb_Y8

The car has been bugged by Amy, who is listening in. She's already at the Lakeside cottage holiday home and she is thinking, good question. Amy sings it back albeit edits the wording somewhat…

"What does it all mean??? What will I see??? If I look closer into all of this bollocks?"

Amy continues to listen in and thinks to herself… I will be writing a frigging long-story about all of this crackpot, nutjob, mind-blowing bollocks, Alice in Wonderland batshit crazy inflated grandiose bullshit on stilts nonsense. She then thinks that would be an appropriate answer to the question What are you going to call your long book? Long book with a long but appropriate title. She could just repeat the title for the synopsis and each chapter of the book could be one of the words in the title of the book… for example CHAPTER 1: Crackpot CHAPTER 2: Nutjob CHAPTER 3: Mind-blowing bollocks CHAPTER 4: Alice in Wonderland batshit crazy inflated grandiose bullshit on stilts nonsense.

Furthermore Amy was a tad flustered that all of this mess had distracted her from her job at the City University of New York. She was behind on marking students papers. She will simply have to tell the students the truth… I'm behind on marking your essays due to personal problems.

Back in the car… Lara says "Put a song on by Amy."

"Amy can't sing."

"Not your Amy… our Amy. The one about tears is appropriate!"

Tears Dry On Their Own (youtube.com)

"Augmented… play Amy Winehouse's Tears Dry on their Own." The song starts to play.

"When we are back in the Void I want to take our consciousness to Amy Winehouse and get a private performance of Rehab."

Amy Winehouse — Rehab (youtube.com)

The other Amy hearing this laughs her head off and says out-loud "Jenny you need rehabilitation!"

Back in the car Sarah and Lara are discussing marriage. This is something that is another subtle difference from the previous near identical timeline where they were already engaged by now. But they already are cosmically married in their minds now. They turn their attention to loved ones here. They feel sorry for everyone here. Sarah says

"They are about to be cured."

"Yeah they shall be. And as for us we are special. Especially together. I mean we are so connected its like we are One… so you aren't an identification. You are part of me" responds Lara.

"Well put."

"What's the plan?" asks Lara. "Because its time Amy heard this."

"… we have left earth. Destination = the Void."

On hearing that Amy broke into tears. She interpreted it correctly as a suicide pact. She now hated Lara even more. She wanted her gone out of Sarah's life. As for Amy's view of Sarah… she wanted her sectioned. And Amy is thinking, what did they mean by saying that I needed to hear this?

Ironically given recent events Amy's plan was to drug them both, to weaken them. At first they would just go to sleep… but on awakening they would be physically weak for a couple of hours so would have no choice but to be compliant. But then Amy hears Sarah and Lara say something that shocks the living daylights out of her. She hears Sarah say the following…

"Amy, I know you are listening. We know that the car is bugged. We know you bugged the house. A neighbour saw you come into my house and into my car… and in chit chat with us mentioned it. So I checked the house and car and noticed the bugs. We are going to prove to you that we are real. At 1pm U.S. Eastern time tomorrow there will be giant UFOs hovering over New York City, London, Toronto, Melbourne and Paris. We are not going to the holiday home… that was to fool you. But we are glad you are free of breast cancer and we know you think we are insane. But know this… you will believe us at 1pm Eastern tomorrow. Love you Amy. Take care. And when you see those UFOs you will know that I am ok. Please ensure that everyone is aware of this message of ours so that everyone who cares about us is aware that we are ok once they have seen the UFO's."

Amy wept.

Sarah and Lara walked into Grand Central Station. They headed for Platform 9. They stepped onto the tracks. The works train hit them at 63 miles per hour vanquishing their body shell and physical brain. Their consciousness was released and they simply felt blissfully in-love.

7. UFO Close Encounters

The next day Amy Barker is sat at home. She isn't doing any work. She has phoned in sick. She feels deeply disturbed and distressed by her friends suicide. She is in a very bad place mentally. She is sat in her office room at her home with her head in her hands and she is sobbing.

It is 12.56pm. But Amy doesn't give a damn about the closeness in time to the so-called multiple UFO close encounters across cities event that is supposed to happen. She thinks it is about as likely to occur as the Loch Ness Monster calling round for a chat. Instead at this moment in time she is thinking about Jenny's collapse. How can she go from a smart, successful, well off and rational adult woman to someone who suddenly makes up a new name for herself and believes all these crazy stories about the Void and so on with such certainty that she is willing to throw herself in-front of a train? The transformation all happened so quickly that Amy thinks it prevented her from getting her friend sectioned. How on earth did that woman, Natalie James, manage to cast such a spell over her? On the one hand Amy blames Natalie and on the other hand she doesn't understand how her friend, who she deemed a professional just last week, could become possessed by her overnight.

Then at 1.01pm she received a phone call from Pete.

"Turn on the News."

"Ok"

Amy says " Augmented, News, CNN"… and a screen appears in-front of her eyes. The screen is split into five sections… so as to show the viewer giant UFOs hovering over (1) New York City, (2) London, (3) Toronto, (4) Melbourne and (5) Paris. All five UFO's are close up, hovering low over their famous cities.

To put it mildly Amy is shocked. She ends the phone-call and shouts

"F**K ME BACKWARDS!!!"

And then a giant UFO appeared right outside Amy's window. She walked up to the window. She could see nothing else. There was just a giant UFO there. It was just hovering. It remained there for 15 minutes. Amy stared at it, gobsmacked for most of the 15 minutes, only turning away from it to look at the images of the other UFO's hovering over the five cities. After 15 minutes the giant UFO outside her window suddenly blinked out of existence akin to switching off a light. Then she could see hundreds of people gathered outside her house. Not surprisingly they had been attracted like moths to light by the huge UFO outside her home. Amy is astonished. She opens her front door and shouts

"Excuse me. Are the New York Times here?"

A guy makes his way through the crowd. Amy says

"Identification please."

The reporter, Ian Elliot, proves he is with the NYT and she invites him into her home.

Amy handed over recordings of Sarah and Lara's conversations. The reporter was instantly astonished at Sarah and Lara's statements made the previous day where they said that they would make these UFO's appear over these five cities at 1 oclock. And the reporter also noted that the two women had said that these UFO's navigate and connect earth bound consciousness with Void consciousness.

"Connecting the land of the living with the world of the dead! WOW WOW WOW!!!" said the reporter.

All of this results in this universe, the most sceptical minded of all the universes that Sarah and Lara had ever encountered, being the one that most thoroughly embraces the UFO Phenomenon as reality.

With the State discredited on this timeline, what would have been a Presidential Disclosure in the past, became one of Disclosure from two figures from outside of that world, by relations of David Attenborough and Morgan Freeman. These relations were almost as well respected as their older family members had been when they were alive… not that death has any meaning now. All is life. The Disclosure location is not the U.S. nor the UK… it is delivered in Toronto, Canada. Attenborough and Morgan say a few words that they thought important emphasising looking after earth and people coming together as One. But most of their Disclosure is, as a President would have done, just saying what U.S. Intelligence has told them to say. However, on this timeline there are no crash retrievals or reverse engineered craft. There are no secretive special access Programs that had been covered up. So instead what we got was a Sarah Aston and Lara Hine Disclosure. Their names were mentioned as was Amy Barkers. This is a

Disclosure about UFOs that connect this world and the next world… the next world being the Void.

Disclosure had a huge impact. It motivated innovators to work out how to create the connecting technology that united this world with the other world. Only a few years later and success! This universe became the only one that Sarah and Lara know of that is able to track consciousness into the afterlife. This totally eliminated the concept of death… all fully achieved by the year 2066. This is 99% healthy as post-traumatic stress disorder and the agony associated with loss instantly became a problem solved. Those horrible conditions were instantly confined to mental health history books. The 1% problem involved a tiny fraction of societies population that used to be motivated to evolve in the here-and-now due to the thought of death. But really, in the past, almost everyone stuck themselves in ego mindset's and didn't get motivated to evolve by the prospect of death. Sarah and Lara had learned this. In their mind humans are about as likely to cease their ego mindstate as dogs are to cease barking. It is also worth noting that this Universe became the only one Sarah and Lara know of that could track consciousness into another timeline. So for example if someone died and then that person transferred their consciousness into another timeline then that consciousness, despite existing in a parallel universe, was tracked. Eventually near identical timelines were also made aware of the potential to track consciousness beyond earthly life. This came about due to the fact that people from the timeline we have seen here learning from the methods of Sarah and Lara, and helping other timelines people to become aware of their potential for scientific and spiritual advancement.

As for Amy Barker… she became very famous overnight as not only did she get a personal visit by a huge UFO on that infamous day… it was also recognized that without her recordings the world would never have connected this earth world with the afterlife… and all of the unnecessary trauma would have simply continued on and on for decades or centuries to come.

Sarah and Lara watched on, transferring their consciousness to this universe. They were delighted with what they had done here. Their personal love for one another was stronger than ever and they had cured unnecessary suffering involving death related trauma. In the first few days of their return to the Void they felt overwhelmed with happiness and joy for the good work they had done, advancing humanity scientifically, spiritually, psychologically, curing trauma and knowing that others were already liberating people on other similar timelines. True bliss.

Whenever Amy Barker was described as a legend she would always remember to respond with something along the lines of …

"No! The true legends are Sarah Aston and Lara Hine."

THE END.

OTHER BOOKS BY PAUL BUDDING (Available to purchase on Amazon)

Book 1 in the Series: Abduction Inspired UFO Disclosure is only the Start

Sarah Aston is falling out of love with her husband, Mike, and at the same time she is having strange nightmares or maybe, actual UFO abductions. Her best friend, the scheming Lara Hine, who wants Sarah for herself as her girlfriend, gets her wish and both she and Sarah then experience shared UFO related contact phenomena.

Indeed, it would seem much of the worlds population are becoming experiencers. This leads to Disclosure of some exotic Other intelligence although it remains unclear what the exact origins of the exotic Others are. (For example, ETs? Simulators? Time Travelers? Interdimensionals?) Lara certainly knows much more than she admits. Eventually she starts to talk. But is she telling the truth?

https://www.amazon.co.uk/Abduction-Inspired-Disclosure-only-Start/dp/B0CN59LKJR/ref=sr_1_1?crid=19FH96TS51Y2D&keywords=abduction+inspired+ufo+disclosure+paul+budding&qid=1700306266&s=books&sprefix=abduction+inspired+ufo+disclosure+paul+budding%2Cstripbooks%2C116&sr=1-1

Book 2 in the Series: The Void

Sarah Aston and Lara Hine are now dead. But consciousness continues in the Void… a terrifying experience at first. But there's nothing to be scared of as it is a place of reflection. Its also a place of creation. And indeed consciousness can experience events from human earthly life. They can transfer their consciousness to any place and any time. She can then witness the event although others there cannot see the consciousness that is watching them. One must keep in mind though that if they regress to far backwards as opposed to reflecting and raising their consciousness… then there are cosmic consequences.

https://www.amazon.co.uk/Void-Mr-Paul-Budding/dp/B0CR81D3B3/ref=sr_1_1?crid=3TRMUD53BEBZ1&dib=eyJ2IjoiMSJ9.ffuUu9DIQfzny_GsH_5kGSLt-L9Pu1QhemoNnxfB7CXfwlXJQCNHMH-F7chYtEeg.FyG3jgpHIWcEbHElC7rowDZx6LFZc1lT7ldQNAf25wg&dib_tag=se&keywords=the+void+paul+budding&qid=1705085492&s=books&sprefix=the+void+paul+budding%2Cstripbooks%2C148&sr=1-1

Review of Book 1: Abduction inspired UFO Disclosure is only the Start.

Paul Budding

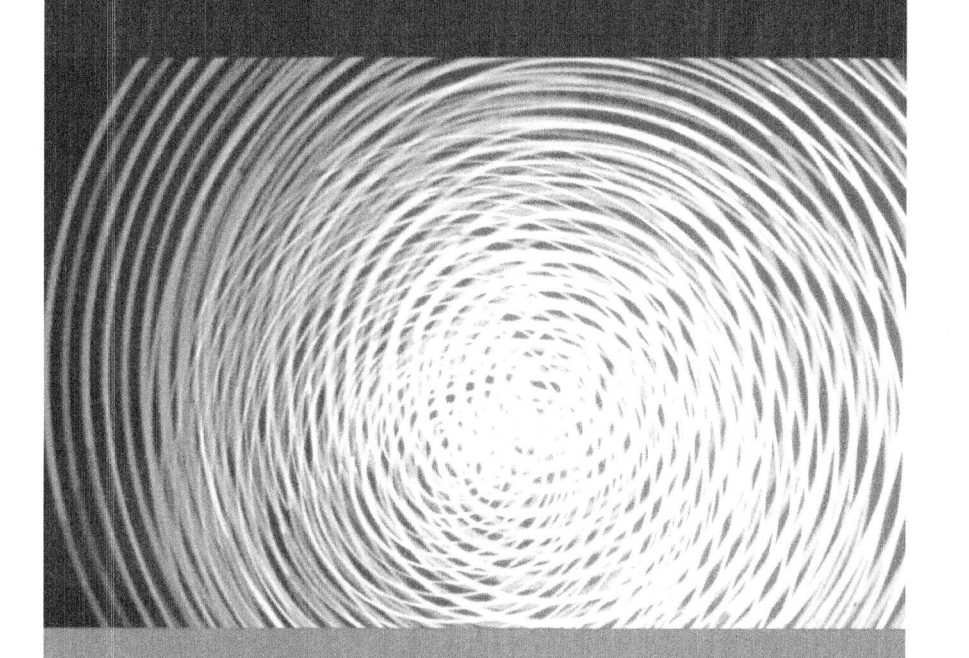

Abduction Inspired UFO Disclosure is only the Start

4.0 out of 5 stars This Book Has Epic Potential

Reviewed by Stewart Bint on 29 November 2023

I originally read this four-chapter book out of order. By that, I mean, chapters three and four before one and two. Why, I hear you ask?

Author Paul Budding had asked if I would take a look at his two short stories, published on an open writers website. They were to become chapters three and four of his 29,000-word book, Abduction Inspired UFO Disclosure is Only the Start.

I was totally intrigued by the concept of his stories, so I went on to read the whole book, which was supplied to me free of charge by the author, in exchange for an honest review.

The overall sci-fi and conspiracy theory story arc is epic, and as far as I know, unique. I'm giving it four stars, having deducted one on two counts.

First: prolific author Jeffrey Archer always says: "Don't call me a writer, because I'm not. I'm a storyteller." And Paul Budding is definitely a fine storyteller with a fine story to tell. But I'd have preferred to see much more 'show' instead of tell. More 'show' would have added better writing to that storyteller tag.

Second: While the concept of this book is a completely new sweeping idea, I personally think the author is missing a huge trick by restricting this mammoth saga to such a short novel.

I believe the author has the idea and potential material for a multi-book series of full-length novels. And by full-length, I mean three books of between 80,000 and 100,000 words each.

Chapters one and two could combine and be expanded to become the first full-length novel introducing the two central characters, showing how they meet and fall in love. This would allow intricate world-building, showing, rather than telling readers, how the UFO Post-Disclosure World came about.

With expansion and development, the third chapter, Lara The Flawed Genius, could become a second full-length novel, with the fourth chapter developing into the final book of the trilogy.

The world-building we have in Abduction Inspired UFO Disclosure is Only the Start is superb, but there is so much untapped story lying beneath the surface.

In my opinion, and remember that's all it is — just my personal opinion — Paul Budding's storytelling is superb, but an editor's eye could tighten up the writing. For example, there's the occasional change of tense from past to present — once even in the same paragraph.

I'd just like to see that full story arc reach its true potential in a trilogy of professionally edited full-length novels.

Having said all this, though, the book as it stands now, fully merits the four stars I've given it, and I thoroughly recommend it to fans of sci-fi and conspiracy theories. Definitely one to get your teeth into.

*NOTE: THE FOLLOWING BOOK IS **NOT** PART OF THE SERIES INVOLVING THE CHARACTERS SARH AND LARA.*

147

Emily Walsh has a natural talent for snooker. Indeed she is a genius. This is despite not ticking the usual boxes that people expect great snooker players to fit into. She is young, American and female. She is also a neurotic. As a child she had symptoms consistent with extreme autism. Her obsessive focus on snooker prevented her from making friends with other girls but also ensured that her potential talent came to the fore. By the time she's 18 she is more bi-polar than autistic although she has never been diagnosed. She craves mental health and she craves to become the number 1 greatest snooker player of all-time. To do the latter she would have to win the World Championship at the Crucible in Sheffield. Walsh' journey from an autistic like existence to stardom is played out within the context of the Post Disclosure World.

https://www.amazon.co.uk/147-Paul-Budding/dp/B0CPSC7MD2/ref=sr_1_1?crid=1NHBUXQQW4NUZ&dib=eyJ2IjoiMSJ9.C0c5yt9EYDmvbODUXL

p08Q.sOUvIRgv4jgUiQysdMGMdIEoajWzOcuJVsfniKwFTdg&dib_tag=se&keywords=147+paul+budding&qid=1705154688&s=books&sprefix=147+paul+budding%2Cstripbooks%2C102&sr=1-1

Contact Paul Budding by email… feel free to contact for information about upcoming books.

paulbudding@yahoo.co.uk

Printed in Great Britain
by Amazon

BULLETPOINTS

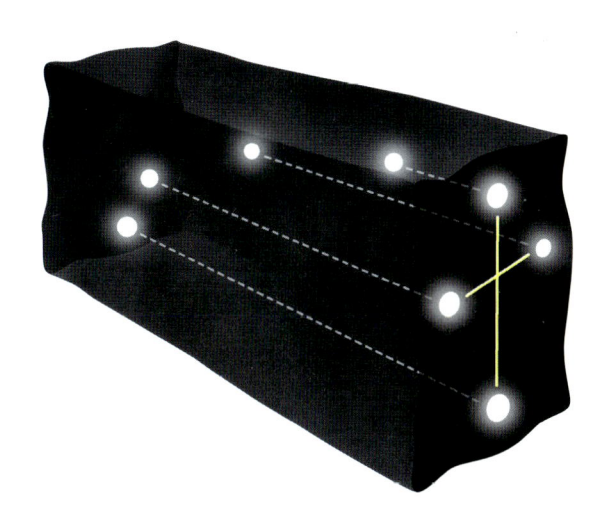

STARS

John Farndon
Consultant: Tim Furniss

Miles Kelly PUBLISHING

First published by Miles Kelly Publishing Ltd
Bardfield Centre, Great Bardfield
Essex, CM7 4SL

Copyright © 2003 Miles Kelly Publishing
Some material in this book first appeared in *1000 Things You Should Know*

2 4 6 8 10 9 7 5 3

Editor
Belinda Gallagher

Design
Andy Knight

Picture Research
Liberty Newton

Inputting
Carol Danenbergs

All rights reserved. No part of this publication may be reproduced, stored in a retrieval system, or transmitted by any means, electronic, mechanical, photocopying, recording or otherwise, without the prior permission of the copyright holder.

British Library Cataloguing-in-Publication Data
A catalogue record for this book is available from the British Library

ISBN 1-84236-237-2

Printed in China

www.mileskelly.net
info@mileskelly.net

The publishers would like to thank the following artists who have contributed to this book:

Kuo Kang Chen, Rob Jakeway, Janos Marffy, Rob Sheffield, Mike White

The publishers would also like to thank NASA for the generous loan of their photographs

Contents

Space catalogues 4

Stars 6

Star charts 8

Constellations 10

Galaxies 12

The Milky Way 14

Nebulae 16

Star birth 18

Giant stars 20

Supernova 22

Dwarf stars 24

Variable stars 26

Neutron stars 28

Pulsars 30

Binary stars 32

Star brightness 34

H–R diagram 36

Celestial sphere 38

Index 40

Space catalogues

- **Astronomers list the stars** in each constellation according to their brightness, using the Greek alphabet (see constellations). So the brightest star in the constellation of Pegasus is Alpha Pegasi.

- **The first catalogue of non-stellar** objects (things other than stars, such as nebulae) was made by astronomer Charles Messier (1730-1817). Objects were named M (for Messier) plus a number. M1 is the Crab nebula.

- **Messier published a list** of 103 objects in 1781, and by 1908 his catalogue had grown to 15,000 entries.

- **Many of the objects** originally listed by Messier as nebulae are now known to be galaxies.

- **Today the standard list of non-stellar objects** is the New General Catalogue of nebulae and star clusters (NGC). First published in 1888, this soon ran to over 13,000 entries.

- **Many objects** are in both the Messier and the NGC and therefore have two numbers.

- **The Andromeda galaxy** is M31 and NGC224.

- **Radio sources** are listed in similar catalogues, such as Cambridge University's 3C catalogue.

- **The first quasar** to be discovered was 3c 48.

- **Many pulsars** are now listed according to their position by right ascension and declination (see celestial sphere).

Stars

▲ *With such an infinite number of stars, galaxies and nebulae in the night sky, astronomers need very detailed catalogues so they can locate each object reliably and check whether it has already been investigated.*

Stars

- **Stars are balls** of mainly hydrogen and helium gas.
- **Nuclear reactions** in the heart of stars, like those in atom bombs, generate heat and light.
- **The heart of a star** reaches 16 million°C. A grain of sand this hot would kill someone 150 km away.
- **The gas in stars** is in a special hot state called plasma, which is made of atoms stripped of electrons.
- **In the core of a star,** hydrogen nuclei fuse (join together) to form helium. This nuclear reaction is called a proton-proton chain.
- **Stars twinkle** because we see them through the wafting of the Earth's atmosphere.
- **Astronomers work out how big a star is** from its brightness and its temperature.
- **The size and brightness** of a star depends on its mass – that is, how much gas it is made of. Our Sun is a medium-sized star, and no star has more than 100 times the Sun's mass or less than 6-7% of its mass.
- **The coolest stars,** such as Arcturus and Antares, glow reddest. Hotter stars are yellow and white. The hottest are blue-white, like Rigel and Zeta Puppis.
- **The blue supergiant Zeta Puppis** has a surface temperature of 40,000°C, while Rigel's is 10,000°C.

▲ *The few thousand stars visible to the naked eye are just a tiny fraction of the trillions in the Universe.*

Stars

▲ *A swarm, or large cluster of stars known as M80 (Nac 6093), from The Milky Way galaxy. This swarm, 28,000 light-years from Earth, contains hundreds of thousands of stars, 'attracted' to each other by gravity.*

Star charts

- **Plotting the positions** of the stars in the sky is a complex business because there are a vast number of them, all at hugely different distances.

- **The first modern star charts** were the German Bonner Durchmusterung (BD) charts of 1859, which show positions of 324,189 stars. *Durchmusterung* means 'scanning through'.

- **The AGK1 chart** of the German Astronomical was completed in 1912 and showed 454,000 stars.

- **The AGK charts** are now on version AGK3 and remain the standard star chart. They are compiled from photographs.

- **The measurements** of accurate places for huge numbers of stars depends on the careful determination of 1,535 stars in the Fundamental Catalog (FK3).

- **Photometric catalogues** map the stars by magnitude and colour, as well as by position.

- **Photographic atlases** do not plot positions of stars on paper, but include photos of them in place.

- **Three main atlases** are popular with astronomers – Norton's Star Atlas, which plots all stars visible to the naked eye; the Tirion Sky Atlas; and the photographic Photographischer Stern-Atlas.

8

Stars

● **Celestial coordinates** are the figures that plot a star's position on a ball-shaped graph (see celestial sphere). The altazimuth system of coordinates gives a star's position by its altitude (its angle in degrees from the horizon) and its azimuth (its angle in degrees clockwise around the horizon, starting from north). The ecliptic system does the same, using the ecliptic rather than the horizon as a starting point. The equatorial system depends on the celestial equator, and gives figures called right ascensions and declination, just like latitude and longitude on Earth.

> FASCINATING FACT
> The star patterns we call constellations were the basis of the first star charts, dating back to the 2nd millennium BC. Even today astronomers divide the sky into 88 constellations, whose patterns are internationally recognized – even though the names of many constellations are the mythical ones given to them by the astronomers of ancient Greece.

◀ *The basic map of the sky shows the 88 constellations that are visible at some time during the year from each hemisphere (half) of the world. This picture shows the northern constellations visible in December.*

Constellations

- **Constellations are patterns** of stars in the sky which astronomers use to help them pinpoint individual stars.
- **Most of the constellations** were identified long ago by the stargazers of Ancient Babylon and Egypt.
- **Constellations are simply patterns** – there is no real link between the stars whatsoever.
- **Astronomers today** recognize 88 constellations.
- **Heroes and creatures** of Greek myth, such as Orion the Hunter and Perseus, provided the names for many constellations, although each name is usually written in its Latin form, not Greek.
- **The stars in each constellation** are named after a letter of the Greek alphabet.
- **The brightest star** in each constellation is called the Alpha star, the next brightest Beta, and so on.
- **Different constellations** become visible at different times of year, as the Earth travels around the Sun.
- **Southern hemisphere constellations** are different from those in the north.
- **The constellation of the Great Bear** – also known by its Latin name Ursa Major – contains an easily recognizable group of seven stars called the Plough or the Big Dipper.

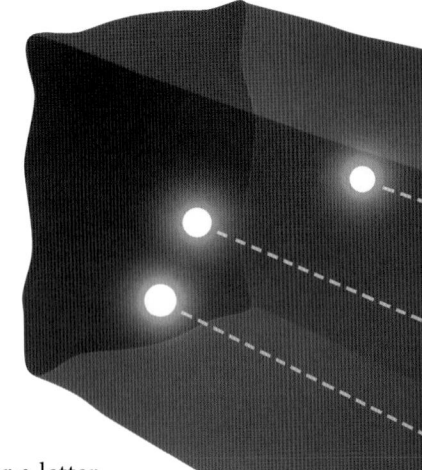

Stars

same star pattern
seen side on

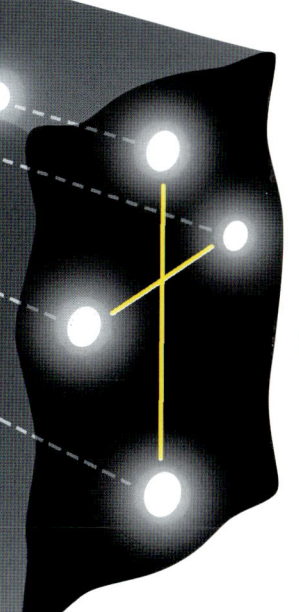

arrow indicates view
seen from Earth

▲ Seen from Earth, the stars in a constellation appear to be the same distance away. In fact they are scattered in space. This diagram shows the relative distances of stars in the Southern Cross constellation.

▲ Constellations are patterns of stars. These help astronomers locate stars among the thousands in the night sky.

11

Galaxies

- **Galaxies are giant groups** of millions or even trillions of stars. Our own local galaxy is the Milky Way.
- **There may be 20 trillion** galaxies in the Universe.
- **Only three galaxies** are visible to the naked eye from Earth besides the Milky Way – the Large and Small Magellanic clouds, and the Andromeda galaxy.
- **Although galaxies are vast,** they are so far away that they look like fuzzy clouds. Only in 1916 did astronomers realize that they are huge star groups.
- **Spiral galaxies** are spinning, Catherine-wheel-like galaxies with a dense core and spiralling arms.
- **Barred spiral galaxies** have just two arms. These are linked across the galaxy's middle by a bar from which they trail like water from a spinning garden sprinkler.
- **Elliptical galaxies** are vast, very old, egg-shaped galaxies, made up of as many as a trillion stars.
- **Irregular galaxies** are galaxies with no obvious shape. They may have formed from the debris of galaxies that crashed into each other.
- **Galaxies are often** found in groups called clusters. One cluster may have 30 or so galaxies in it.

▶ *Like our own Milky Way and the nearby Andromeda galaxy, many galaxies are spiral in shape, with a dense core of stars and long, whirling arms made up of millions of stars.*

FASCINATING FACT
Galaxies like the Small Magellanic Cloud may be the debris of mighty collisions between galaxies.

The Milky Way

▲ *The spiralling Milky Way galaxy looks much like a Catherine wheel firework.*

- **The Milky Way** is the faint, hazy band of light that you can see stretching right across the night sky.
- **Looking through binoculars,** you would see that the Milky Way is made up of countless stars.
- **A galaxy** is a vast group of stars, and the Milky Way is the galaxy we live in.
- **There are billions** of galaxies in space.
- **The Milky Way** is 100,000 light-years across and 1000 light-years thick. It is made up of 100 billion stars.
- **All the stars** are arranged in a spiral (like a giant Catherine wheel), with a bulge in the middle.
- **Our Sun** is just one of the billions of stars on one arm of the spiral.
- **The Milky Way** is whirling rapidly, spinning our Sun and all its other stars around at 100 million km/h.

Stars

- **The Sun** travels around the galaxy once every 200 million years – a journey of 100,000 light-years.
- **The huge bulge** at the centre of the Milky Way is about 20,000 light-years across and 3000 thick. It contains only very old stars and little dust or gas.
- **There may be a huge black hole** in the very middle of the Milky Way.

▼ *To the naked eye, the Milky Way looks like a hazy, white cloud, but binoculars show it to be a blur of countless stars.*

Nebulae

- **Nebula** (plural nebulae) was the word once used for any fuzzy patch of light in the night sky. Nowadays, many nebulae are known to be galaxies instead.
- **Many nebulae** are gigantic clouds of gas and space dust.
- **Glowing nebulae** are named because they give off a dim, red light, as the hydrogen gas in them is heated by radiation from nearby stars.
- **The Great Nebula of Orion** is a glowing nebula just visible to the naked eye.
- **Reflection nebulae** have no light of their own. They can only be seen because starlight shines off the dust in them.
- **Dark nebulae** not only have no light of their own, they also soak up all light. They can only be seen as patches of darkness, blocking out light from the stars behind them.

▲ *This is a glowing nebula called the Lagoon nebula, which glows as hydrogen and helium gas in it is heated by radiation from stars.*

Stars

- **The Horsehead nebula** in Orion is the best-known dark nebula. As its name suggests, it is shaped like a horse's head.
- **Planetary nebulae** are thin rings of gas cloud which are thrown out by dying stars. Despite their name, they have nothing to do with planets.
- **The Ring nebula** in Lyra is the best-known of the planetary nebulae.
- **The Crab nebula** is the remains of a supernova that exploded in AD 1054.

▲ *There are two general types of nebulae. Diffuse nebulae, the larger of the two, can contain enough dust and gases to form 100,000 stars the size of the Sun. Planetary nebulae form when a dying star throws off the outer layers of its atmosphere.*

Star birth

- **Stars are being born** and dying all over the Universe, and by looking at stars in different stages of their life, astronomers have worked out their life stories.
- **Medium-sized stars** last for about ten billion years. Small stars may last for 200 billion years.
- **Big stars** have short, fierce lives of ten million years.
- **Stars start life** in clouds of gas and dust called nebulae.
- **Inside nebulae,** gravity creates dark clumps called dark nebulae, each clump containing the seeds of a family of stars.
- **As gravity squeezes** the clumps in dark nebulae, they become hot.
- **Smaller clumps** never get very hot and eventually fizzle out. Even if they start burning, they lose surface gas and shrink to wizened, old white dwarf stars.
- **If a larger clump** reaches 10 million °C, hydrogen atoms in its core begin to join together in nuclear reactions, and the baby star starts to glow.
- **In a medium-sized star** like our Sun, the heat of burning hydrogen pushes gas out as fiercely as gravity pulls inwards, and the star becomes stable (steady).
- **Medium-sized stars** burn steadily until all of their hydrogen fuel is used up.

▶ *Stars are born within clouds of gas and dust (nebulae).*

19

Giant stars

- **Giant stars** are 10 to 100 times as big as the Sun, and 10 to 1000 times as bright.

- **Red giants** are stars that have swollen 10 to 100 times their size, as they reach the last stages of their life and their outer gas layers cool and expand.

- **Giant stars have burned** all their hydrogen, and so burn helium, fusing (joining) helium atoms to make carbon.

- **The biggest stars** go on swelling after they become red giants, and grow into supergiants.

- **Supergiant stars** are up to 500 times as big as the Sun, with absolute magnitudes of -5 to -10 (see star brightness).

- **Pressure in the heart** of a supergiant is enough to fuse carbon atoms together to make iron.

▲ *A red supergiant is an enormous star, 500 times the diameter of the Sun.*

- **All the iron in the Universe** was made in the heart of supergiant stars.

- **There is a limit to the brightness** of supergiants, so they can be used as distance markers by comparing how bright they look to how bright they are (see distances).

- **Supergiant stars** eventually collapse and explode as supernovae.

Stars

▼ *The constellation of Cygnus, the Swan, contains the very biggest star in the known Universe – a hypergiant which is almost a million times as big as the Sun.*

FASCINATING FACT
The biggest-known star is the hypergiant Cygnus OB2 No.12, which is 810,000 times as bright as the Sun.

Supernova

- **A supernova** (plural supernovae) is the final, gigantic explosion of a supergiant star at the end of its life.

- **A supernova** lasts for just a week or so, but shines as bright as a galaxy of 100 billion ordinary stars.

- **Supernovae happen** when a supergiant star uses up its hydrogen and helium fuel and shrinks, boosting pressure in its core enough to fuse heavy elements such as iron (see nuclear energy).

- **When iron begins to fuse** in its core, a star collapses instantly – then rebounds in a mighty explosion.

- **Seen in 1987, supernova 1987A** was the first viewed with the naked eye since Kepler's 1604 sighting.

- **Supernova remnants** (leftovers) are the gigantic, cloudy shells of material swelling out from supernovae.

- **A supernova** seen by Chinese astronomers in AD 184 was thought to be such a bad omen that it sparked off a palace revolution.

- **A dramatic supernova** was seen by Chinese astronomers in AD 1054 and left the Crab nebula.

- **Elements heavier** than iron were made in supernovae.

▶ *Seeing a supernova is rare, but at any moment in time there is one happening somewhere in the Universe.*

Stars

FASCINATING FACT
Many of the elements that make up your body were forged in supernovae.

Dwarf stars

- **Dwarf stars are small stars** of low brightness (see H-R diagram). But even though they are small, they contain a large amount of matter.

- **Red dwarves** are bigger than the planet Jupiter but smaller than our medium-sized star, the Sun. They glow faintly, with 0.01% of the Sun's brightness.

- **No red dwarf** can be seen with the naked eye – not even the nearest star to the Sun, the red dwarf Proxima Centauri.

- **White dwarves** are the last stage in the life of a medium-sized star. Although they are even smaller than red dwarves – no bigger than the Earth – they contain the same amount of matter as the Sun.

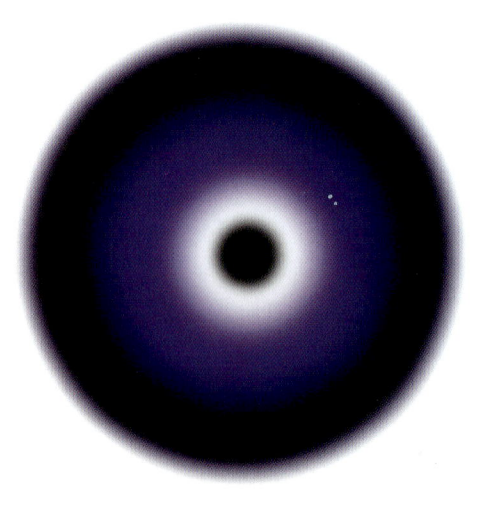

▲ *Black dwarves are stars that were either not big enough to start shining, or which have burned up all their nuclear fuel and stopped glowing, like a coal cinder.*

- **Our night sky's brightest star,** Sirius, the Dog Star, has a white dwarf companion called the Pup Star.

- **The white dwarf Omicron-2 Eridani** (also called 40 Eridani) is one of the few dwarf stars that can be seen from the Earth with the naked eye.

Stars

- **Brown dwarves** are very cool space objects, little bigger than Jupiter.
- **Brown dwarves** formed in the same way as other stars, but were not big enough to start shining properly. They just glow very faintly with the heat left over from their formation.
- **Black dwarves** are very small, cold, dead stars.
- **The smallest kind of star** is called a neutron star.

▲ *A star's life-cycle shows five typical stages, from gas and dust collecting to a small, hot, white dwarf.*

Variable stars

- **Variable stars** are stars that do not burn steadily like our Sun, but which flare up and down.
- **Pulsating variables** are stars that pulse almost as if they were breathing. They include the kinds of star known as Cepheid variables and RR Lyrae variables.
- **Cepheid variables** are big, bright stars that pulse with energy, flaring up regularly every 1 to 100 days.
- **Cepheid variables** are so predictable in brightness that they make good distance markers (see distances).
- **RR Lyrae variables** are yellow, supergiant stars near the end of their life, which flicker as their fuel runs down.
- **Mira-type variables** are similar to Mira in Cetus, the Whale, and vary regularly over months or years.
- **RV Tauri variables** are very unpredictable, flaring up and down over changing periods of time.
- **Eclipsing variables** are really eclipsing binaries (see binary stars). They seem to flare up and down, but in fact are simply one star getting in the way of the other.
- **The Demon Star** is Algol in Perseus. It seems to burn fiercely for 59 hours, become dim, then flare up again ten hours later. It is really an eclipsing binary.
- **The vanishing star** is Chi in Cygnus, the Swan. It can be seen with the naked eye for a few months each year, but then becomes so dim that it cannot be seen, even with a powerful telescope.

▲ *The constellation of Cygnus, containing a vanishing star.*

Stars

▲ *This eerie image is a vast cloud of gas around the Perseus Cluster, millions of light-years from Earth.*

Neutron stars

- **Neutron stars** are incredibly small, super-dense stars made mainly of neutrons (see atoms), with a solid crust made of iron and similar elements.
- **Neutron stars** are just 20 km across on average, yet weigh as much as the Sun.
- **A tablespoon** of neutron star would weigh about ten billion tonnes.
- **Neutron stars** form from the central core of a star that has died in a supernova explosion.
- **A star must be more than** 1.4 times as big as a medium-sized star like our Sun to produce a neutron star. This is the Chandrasekhar limit.
- **A star more than three times** as big as the Sun would collapse beyond a neutron star to form a black hole. This is called the Oppenheimer-Volkoff limit.
- **The first evidence** of neutron stars came when pulsars were discovered in the 1960s.
- **Some stars giving out X-rays,** such as Hercules X-1, may be neutron stars. The X-rays come from material from nearby stars squeezed on to their surfaces by their huge gravity.
- **Neutron stars** have very powerful magnetic fields (see magnetism), over 2000 times stronger than Earth's, which stretch the atoms out into frizzy 'whiskers' on the star's surface.

▲ *Neutron stars are tiny, super-dense stars that form in supernova explosions, as a star's core collapses within seconds under the huge force of its own immense gravity.*

Stars

▲ *Supernova 1987A, photographed from the Hubble space telescope.*

Pulsars

- **A pulsar** is a neutron star that spins rapidly, beaming out regular pulses of radio waves – rather like an invisible cosmic lighthouse.
- **The first pulsar** was detected by a Cambridge astronomer called Jocelyn Bell Burnell in 1967.
- **At first astronomers thought** the regular pulses might be signals from aliens, and pulsars were jokingly called LGMs (short for Little Green Men).
- **Most pulsars** send their radio pulse about once a second. The slowest pulse only every four seconds, and the fastest every 1.6 milliseconds.
- **The pulse rate** of a pulsar slows down as it gets older.
- **The Crab pulsar** slows by a millionth each day.
- **More than 650 pulsars** are now known, but there may be 100,000 active in our galaxy.
- **Pulsars probably result** from a supernova explosion – that is why most are found in the flat disc of the Milky Way, where supernovae occur.
- **Pulsars are not found** in the same place as supernovae because they form after the debris from the explosion has spread into space.
- **We know** they come from tiny neutron stars often less than 10 km across, because they pulse so fast.

▶ The Crab nebula contains a pulsar also known as NP0532. It is the youngest pulsar yet discovered and it probably formed after the supernova explosion seen in the Crab nebula in AD 1054. It has a rotation period of 0.0331 seconds, but it is gradually slowing down.

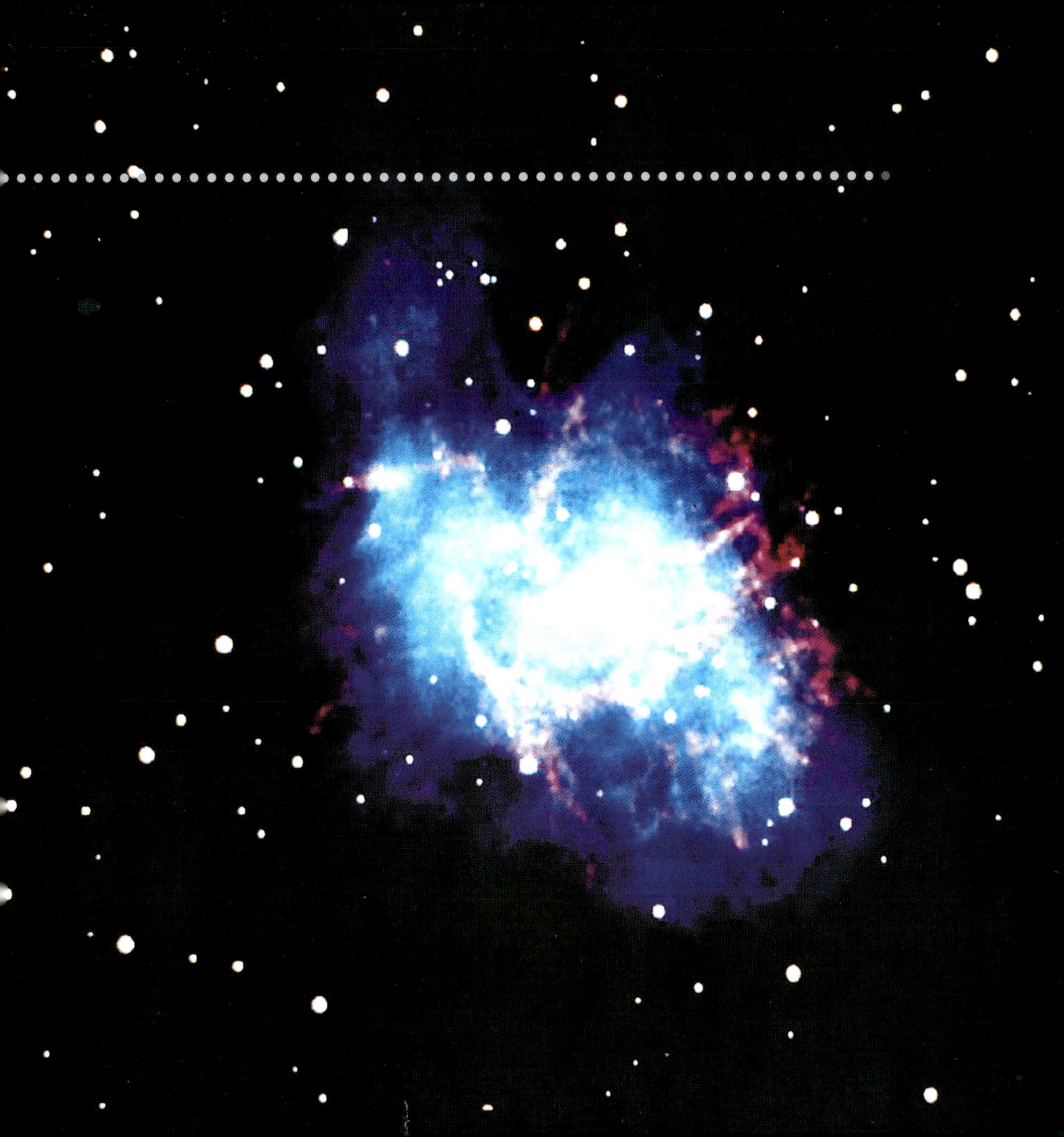

Binary stars

- **Our Sun is alone** in space, but most stars have one, two or more starry companions.

- **Binaries are double stars,** and there are various kinds.

- **True binary stars** are two stars held together by one another's gravity, which spend their lives whirling around together like a pair of dancers.

- **Optical binaries** are not really binaries at all. They are simply two stars that look as if they are together because they are in roughly the same line of sight from the Earth.

▼ *Binary system with similar sized stars. The stars may be close together or millions of kilometres apart.*

▼ *Binary system with much larger star (which is also a red giant).*

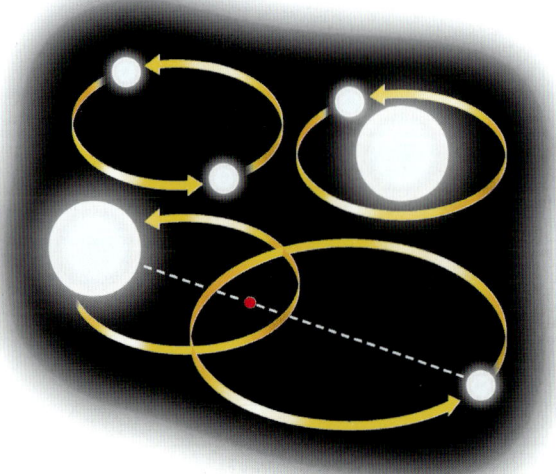

- **Eclipsing binaries** are true binary stars that spin round in exactly the same line of sight from Earth. This means they keep blocking out one another's light.

- **Spectroscopic binaries** are true binaries that spin so closely together that the only way we can tell there are two stars is by changes in colour.

▲ *Stars in a binary system revolve around their common centres of gravity.*

Stars

- **The star Epsilon** in the constellation of Lyra is called the Double Double, because it is a pair of binaries.
- **Mizar, in the Great Bear,** was the first binary star to be discovered.
- **Mizar's companion Alcor** is an optical binary star.
- **Albireo in Cygnus** is an optical binary visible to the naked eye – one star looks gold, the other, blue.

▲ *In the middle of this picture is the constellation of Cygnus, the Swan, which contains an optical binary star called Albireo – a pair of stars that only appear to be partners, but which are in fact some way apart.*

Star brightness

- **Star brightness** is worked out on a scale of magnitude (amount) that was first devised in 150 BC by the Ancient Greek astronomer Hipparchus.
- **The brightest star** Hipparchus could see was Antares, and he described it as magnitude 1. He described the faintest star he could see as magnitude 6.
- **Using telescopes and binoculars,** astronomers can now see much fainter stars than Hipparchus could.
- **Good binoculars** show magnitude 9 stars, while a home telescope will show magnitude 10 stars.
- **Brighter stars than Antares** have been identified with magnitudes of less than 1, and even minus numbers. Betelgeuse is 0.8, Vega is 0.0, and the Sun is -26.7.
- **The brightest-looking star** from Earth is Sirius, the Dog Star, with a magnitude of -1.4.
- **The magnitude scale only** describes how bright a star looks from Earth compared to other stars. This is its relative magnitude.

▲ You can estimate a star's magnitude by comparing its brightness to two stars whose magnitude you do know – one star a little brighter and one a little dimmer.

Stars

- **The further away a star is,** the dimmer it looks and the smaller its relative magnitude is, regardless of how bright it really is.
- **A star's absolute magnitude** describes how bright a star really is.
- **The star Deneb** is 60,000 times brighter than the Sun. But because it is 1800 light-years away, it looks dimmer than Sirius.

▲ *A large telescope will reveal stars as faint as magnitude 10.*

H-R diagram

- **The Hertzsprung-Russell (H-R) diagram** is a graph in which the colour of stars is plotted against their brightness.
- **The colour of a star** depends on its temperature.
- **Cool stars** are red or reddish-yellow.
- **Hot stars** burn white or blue.
- **Medium-sized stars** form a diagonal band called the main sequence across the graph.
- **The whiter and hotter** a main sequence star is, the brighter it shines. White stars and blue-white stars are usually bigger and younger.
- **The redder and cooler** a star is, the dimmer it glows. Cool red stars tend to be smaller and older.
- **Giant stars and dwarf stars** lie to either side of the main sequence stars.
- **The H-R diagram** shows how bright each colour star should be. If the star actually looks dimmer, it must be further away. By comparing the brightness predicted by the H-R diagram against how bright a star really looks, astronomers can work out how far away it is (see distances).
- **The H-R diagram** was devised independently by Ejnar Hertzsprung in 1911 and Henry Russell in 1913.

▶ *The H-R diagram shows the temperature and brightness of different types of stars. It can be used to predict how far away a star is, based on how bright it appears.*

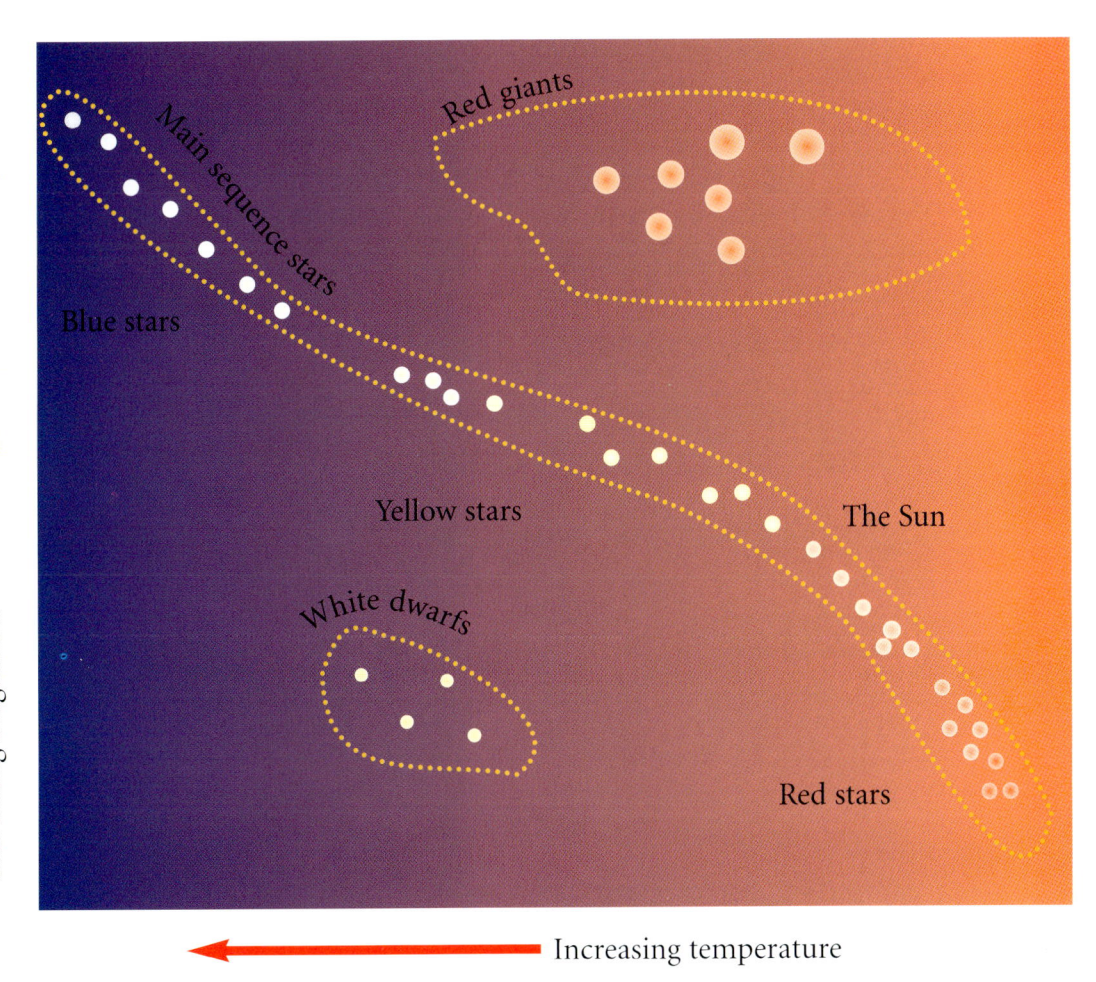

Stars

Celestial sphere

- **Looking at the stars,** they seem to move across the night sky as though they were painted on the inside of a giant, slowly turning ball. This is the celestial sphere.
- **The northern tip** of the celestial sphere is called the North Celestial Pole.
- **The southern tip** is the South Celestial Pole.
- **The celestial sphere rotates** on an axis which runs between its two celestial poles.
- **There is an equator** around the middle of the celestial sphere, just like Earth's.
- **Stars are positioned** on the celestial sphere by their declination and their right ascension.
- **Declination** is like latitude. It is measured in degrees and shows a star's position between pole and equator.
- **Right ascension** is like longitude. It is measured in hours, minutes and seconds, and shows how far a star is from a marker called the First Point of Aries.
- **The Pole Star,** Polaris, lies very near the North Celestial Pole.
- **The zenith** is the point on the sphere directly above your head as you look at the night sky.

▶ *The celestial sphere is like a great blue ball dotted with stars, with the Earth in the middle. It is imaginary, but makes it easy to locate stars and constellations. The zodiac is shown on the inset.*

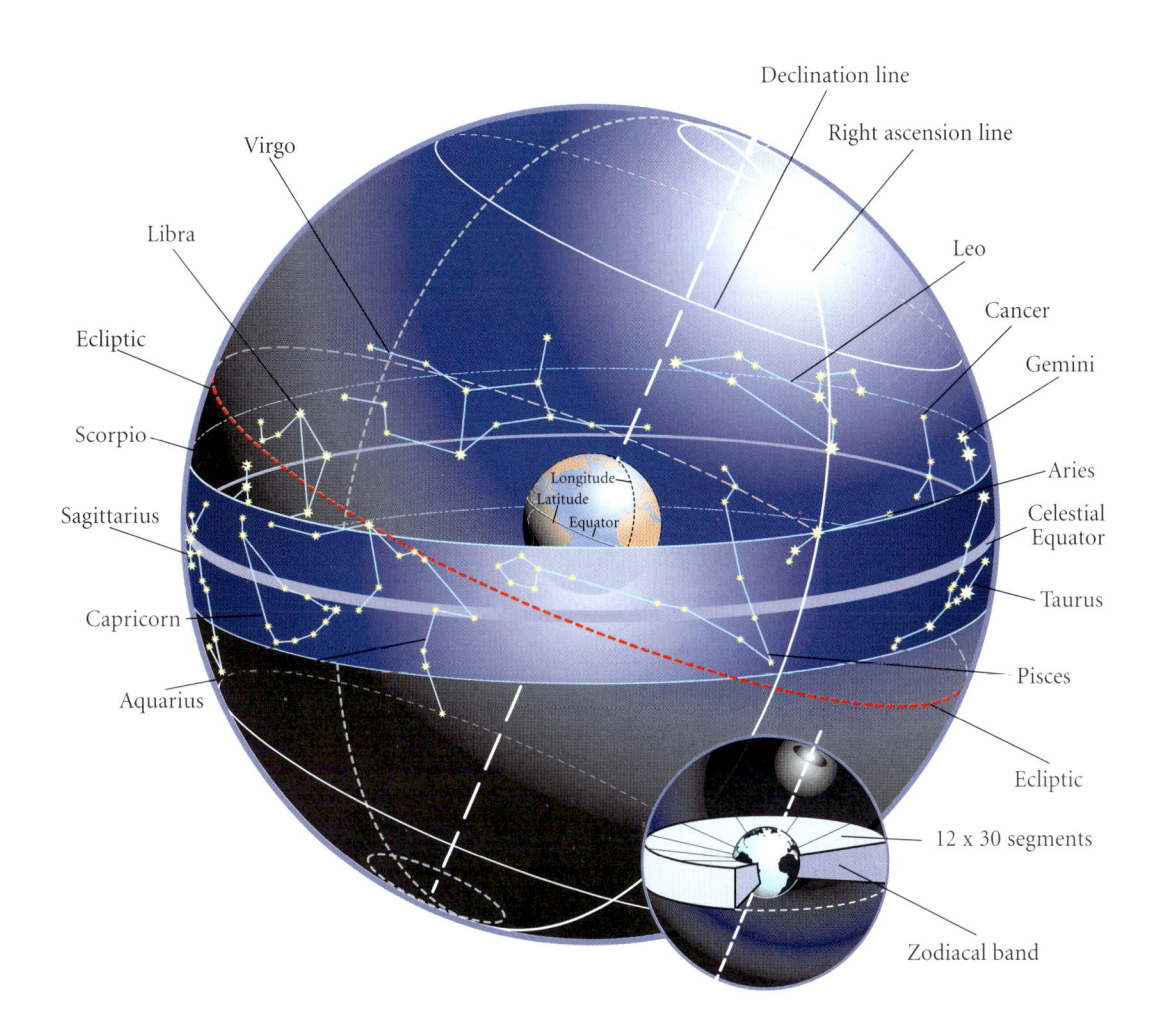

Stars

39

Index

Albireo 33, *33*
Alcor 33
Alpha Pegasi 4
Alpha stars of constellations 10
altitude 9
Andromeda galaxy 4, 12, *12*
Antares 34
Arcturuss 6
axis 38
azimuth 9

barrel spiral galaxy 12
Beta stars of constellations 10
Betelgeuse 34
Big Dipper constellation 10
binary stars 26, **32-33**
black dwarf stars *24*
black holes
    Milky Way 15
    neutron stars 28
brightness **34-35**
brown dwarf stars 25

celestial coordinates 9
celestial sphere 4, **38-39**
Cephid variable stars 26
Cetus 26
Chi 26
clouds 16, 18, *18*, 22, 27
clusters 12
constellations **10-11**
Crab nebula 4, 17, 22, *30*
Crab pulsar 30
Cygnus
    binary stars 33, *33*
    giant stars *21*
    variable stars 26

dark nebulae 16, 17, 18
declination 4, 38
Demon Star 26
Deneb 35
Dog Star 24, 34
dwarf stars **24-25**, 36

eclipsing variable stars 26
eclipsing binary stars 32
ecliptic system 9
elliptical galaxies 12
Epsilon 33

equator, celestial sphere 38
equatorial system 9

First Point of Aries 38
fusion 20

galaxies **12-13**
gas clouds
    nebulae 16, 17, *17*
    Perseus Cluster *27*
    star birth 18, *18*
giant stars **20-21**, 36
gravity
    binary stars 32
    neutron stars 28, *28*
    star birth 18
    star cluster *7*
Great Bear 10, 33
Great Nebula of Orion 16
Greeks 9, 34

helium
    giant stars 20
    nebulae *16*
    stars 6
    supernovae 22
Hercules X-1 neutron star 28
Hertzsprung-Russell diagram **36-37**
Hipparchus of Nicaea 34
Horsehead Nebula 17
Hubble space, supernovae *29*
hydrogen
    giant stars 20
    nebulae 16
    stars 6, 18
    supernovae 22
hypergiant stars 21

irregular galaxies 12

Kepler, Johannes 22

Lagoon nebulae *16*
Large Magellanic Cloud 12
light-years, Milky Way 14, 15
Lyra 17, 33

magnitude
    brightness 34, *34*, 35
    giant stars 20
    star charts 8

mass, stars 6
matter, dwarf stars 24
Milky Way 7, **14-15**
    galaxies 12, *12*
    pulsars 30
Mira-type variable stars 26
Mizar binary stars 33
M80 star cluster *7*

Nac 6093 star cluster *7*
nebulae **16-17**
    space catalogues 4, *4*
    star birth 18 *18*
neutron stars 25, **28-29**, 30
non-stellar objects 4
northern hemisphere
    constellations 9, 10
Norton's Star Atlas 8
nuclear energy 22
nuclear fuel *24*
nuclear fusion 6
nuclear reactions, stars 6, 18

Oppenheimer-Volkoff limit 28
optical binary stars 32, 33, *33*
Orion 10, 16, 17

Pegasus 26
Perseus Cluster *27*
Perseus constellation 10
planetary nebulae 17, *17*
Plow constellation 10
Polaris 38
Pole Star 38
Proxima Centauri 24
pulsars **30-31**
    neutron stars 28
    space catalogues 4
pulsating stars 26
Pup Star 24

radiation, nebulae 16, *16*
radio waves 30
red dwarf stars 24
red giant stars 20, *20*, 32
red stars 36
reflection nebulae 16

Sirius 24, 34, 35
Small Magellanic Cloud 12, 13

Southern Cross constellation *11*
southern hemisphere, constellations 9, 10
spectroscopic binary stars 32
spiral galaxies 12, *12*
    Milky Way 14
star birth **18-19**
star charts **8-9**
star clusters 4, *7*
stars **6-7**
    binary **32-33**
    brightness 34, *34*, 35
    celestial sphere 38, *39*
    constellations 10, *11*
    dwarf **24-25**
    galaxies 12
    H-R diagram 36
    life cycle 25
    Milky Way 14, 15, *15*
    nebulae 16, *16*, 17, *17*
    neutron **28-29**
    space catalogues 4, *4*
    supernovae 22
    variable **26-27**
Sun
    binary stars 32
    brightness 34
    Milky Way 14, 15
    neutron stars 28
    star birth 18
    stars 6
super-dense stars 28, *28*
supergiant stars 6, 20, 22
    variable stars 26
supernovae **22-23**
supernova 1987A 22
Swan *21*, 26, *26*, 33

Ursa major constellation 10

vanishing star 26
variable stars **26-27**

white dwarf stars 18, 24
    star life cycle 25
white stars 36

X-rays, neutron stars 28

zenith 38
zodiac *39*